LOVELADIES ENNUI

BY KESLIE PATCH-BOHROD

Published by Starry Night Publishing.Com

Rochester, New York

Copyright 2021 Keslie Patch-Bohrod

Karen,
Best Wishes and I hope
you enjoy the book!
Keslie Patch-Bohrod

Keslie Patch-Bohrod

AUTHOR'S DISCLAIMER

This is a work of fiction. Any resemblance to actual events or persons, living or dead, is entirely coincidental. Some of the information used in this book surrounding Nathan Silvermaster, William 'Lud' Ullmann and their associates, Project MKUltra and the CIA is true while the rest is a product of the author's imagination. Silvermaster and Ullmann were accused but never convicted of being spies. They are part of the wonderful lore of Loveladies.

Long Beach Island, Loveladies and other towns/cities, and some of the restaurants or businesses mentioned in this book are real but used within a fictional setting. The remaining names, characters, places, and incidents are either a product of the author's imagination or are used fictitiously, and any resemblance to actual persons, living or dead, events or places is entirely coincidental or has nothing to do with their actual conduct.

So if you think this book is about you, it is not. If I were going to write about you, it would be a biography not fiction.

* * * * *

Thank you to Jayne Rutan, Carey Schwartz Roseman, Laurie Mortensen, Sonia Abrahams Hughes and my husband Bill for taking the time to read, edit and suggest changes/additions; to Laurie Simpson Sebastiano for the cover photograph and to my family for their encouragement.

Keslie Patch-Bohrod

CONTENTS

PROLOGUE

1961

Segments from the Lost Memoir of Nathan Gregory Silvermaster

The FBI reportedly called her some pretty unflattering names. I would have called her something else. Traitor, possibly. Not to the United States, but to Russia. I could have killed her if she hadn't already been in the hands of the federal government. Elizabeth Bentley just waltzed right in; she should have kept her mouth shut instead of implicating all of us and trying to cut a deal with the FBI and selling out everyone she knew. Stupid woman. She turned against a cause that she had believed in. Once Jacob Golos, her lover, died she no longer had the desire to work for the Russians. Maybe she felt she should have been given a bigger role instead of being cut loose. Maybe she was afraid of being killed. But instead, she gave the FBI a list of names, lots of names. Lud and I were high on the list. Helen never trusted her but we had no choice, Jacob said we had to work with her. Now look where it had gotten us.

After the Nazis invaded the Soviet Union, we thought it imperative to help provide intelligence to Russia on the German army and their plans. The three of us, Helen, Lud and I were honored to be a part of it. We had to do what we thought best for the war effort. Thankfully, Lud and I were privy to many discussions and plans within the White House in 1941. My career in Washington might have ended earlier if it hadn't been for Lauchlin Curry's help in stopping the inquiries into my membership with the Communist Party of the United States. With no more investigation, I was able to move onto the War Production Board and send on information concerning U.S. arms production. I was informed I would be receiving a medal from the KGB for my hard work. What an honor.

The House Un-American Activities Committee had been relentless in its questioning. Their intent clear: to get our confessions, but we were relentless also in pleading the fifth. Lud and I endured repeated questioning in the late 1940s and early 1950s but I was never prosecuted. However, Lud was called back in 1954 and offered immunity under a new law if he would testify. When they threatened a prison sentence in 1956, he finally gave in and testified. No one would know what he said and thankfully, he was never charged.

At least things had panned out on Long Beach Island. We were able to find a way to earn a living and no one seemed to care who we were or what we had been accused of. The land purchase came through, the dredging completed and the home designs were great. We recouped our initial investment and became financially secure. If we hadn't been able to start our own business we wouldn't have been able to survive. We were drummed out of Washington and the FBI made sure no one would ever hire us because we would always be labeled Soviet spies.

That Pronin boy was a godsend and really pulled his weight. I knew his father, who was a Russian Ambassador in Washington, D.C. I had met him socially at a few government functions where he told me about his son Alek. He asked that I take him under my wing and he promised his son was a strong, committed, young man; and we found that to be true. He was not a real social butterfly but seemed willing to do whatever was needed to get the job done. Lud and I were able to help him arrange a suitable wife from Belarus. With time, he should be an asset to the long term goal. We still have so much to do, the job is not done.

The House Un-American Activities Committee questioning would continue even after Silvermaster and Ullmann left Washington. But that didn't stop them from reinventing themselves and going on with their lives as was evident in their attendance at the Long Beach Island parties. Their contacts were increasing as were the sales of their quaint little lagoon-side homes in Loveladies. They were surviving this storm.

However, their route was in recalculation. Another storm was coming.

It was Ash Wednesday, March 5, 1962 and just your average day, cool with a little rain in the forecast. A few days later, much of the New Jersey Shore would be wiped out.

There was little or no warning of what was to come. It was a powerful Nor'easter that included almost all of the descriptive weather terms including high winds, snow, sleet, hail, and some say the waves topped thirty five feet. Almost the entire island was underwater, from the northern tip at Barnegat Light to almost three quarters of the way down the island to Beach Haven and with it tons of sand was deposited. After three days of wind and water pummeling the island, some houses remained standing, but most were completely destroyed. There was just so much sand and water.

March 7, 1962

Alek Pronin knew the Silvermasters wouldn't be able to get to their house in Harvey Cedars because of the destruction. Thankfully, they had been away at the time of the storm. Having worked for Nathan Silvermaster and William 'Lud' Ullmann in their construction business for years, he thought it was his responsibility to assess the damage and see what he could do to help, possibly something could be salvaged. He lived only a few streets away, thankfully, his house was still standing. There was considerable damage, but he and his wife Alina, would be able to live in it while making the necessary repairs. He wasn't sure about the other houses. Loveladies had been such a beautiful community. He had helped Silvermaster and Ullmann build these homes on the lagoons. Now, he wasn't sure they would be able to rebuild what had once been.

After the storm subsided, he trudged through the water and sand as he made his way down what he thought was the boulevard. It was hard to tell with all the debris. There were a few people out and about now, all seemed to be in shock, but grateful to be alive after the pounding they experienced. He was sure a number of people were dead just by the look of the devastation. Harvey Cedars, the next area over to the south, was almost knocked off from the map.

He moved from house to house surveying the damage and picking up odds and ends. When he finally reached it, there was not much left to the Silvermaster's home, but he did find some papers floating around in the flotsam and jetsam so he gathered up what he could. Much of the home and belongings were destroyed when the storm surge made its way through the house. He would leave the rest of house to the owners to sort through.

When he returned to his own house, Alek carefully laid out the few pages on the kitchen table to dry. Not all of the writing was legible, only a few pages survived the drying process. He had to hold up the papers to the light. He could only make out 5 paragraphs. This must have been portions of his memoirs, thought Alek. He knew he was writing them. The ink was smeared, some sentences were not legible. What he was able to make out left him with a sense of pride and gratefulness. Alek knew he couldn't let Silvermaster or the rest of them down. They had trained him and set him up in Loveladies to begin accumulating information until the day when he would be activated.

He destroyed what was left of Silvermaster's unpublished memoir.

CHAPTER 1

It was a tree like no other; with its full, dense branches that would make rustling sounds with the slightest breeze, sending you into a dream-like trance. It reminded one of the soft golf claps at a tournament or the shushing sound of a mother calming a sobbing child. Sitting or lounging outside within its radius brought about listlessness with no desire to do anything about it. Breathing deepened, body relaxed, eyes closed as the rustling sounds rose and fell like the crescendo and decrescendo in a symphony. Long, lazy summer days were filled with its music. Loveladies ennui would set in. Invitations were extended, but were politely declined. There was no desire to leave the confines of its space. Even the noise from the annoying neighbors could not interfere with its healing touch.

Then they cut it down.

Keslie Patch-Bohrod

CHAPTER 2

Labor Day 2017

Warner "Chicky" Haverford started his day with his usual one mile walk. It was quite early this Labor Day, so he didn't expect to see too many people walking on Long Beach Boulevard. It was the end of summer for the shore towns on Long Beach Island, New Jersey and residents and renters would be packing up their remaining food and belongings and returning to their primary homes. He was glad that was all behind him now that he was semi-retired and living in Loveladies permanently. A computer, phone and internet connection was all he needed to finish up the few remaining cases he had with the CIA.

Reaching the Long Beach Island Foundation of the Arts and Sciences, his halfway point, he pivoted and headed south back toward his home.

A few minutes later, Chicky saw a man approaching him from the other direction, also walking. He had been debating how he could approach and confront this man, and decided to say something to him now.

As they faced each other on the side of the road, Chicky said, "I know you are up to something but I can't figure out what it is yet. But trust me; I'll get to the bottom of it. You have been watched for quite some time and we know you were connected to Silvermaster. I suggest you stop right now and maybe I won't pursue it further. We are both very old men and don't have much time left. Please make the best of the remaining years you have and don't do anything foolish." Chicky walked away from his encounter, leaving the man staring at him. Were his suspicions correct or did he just make a huge mistake by showing his hand?

The intelligence said there was a spy working this area, passing key information to the Russians, but he had no concrete evidence. What that information entailed was also a partial mystery. They knew it was economic in nature and probably linked to the computer hacking and attack on the Ukrainian power grid in 2015. Hackers had been going after every sector within the Ukraine. He feared this activity was only a test, a trial if you will, to something bigger; possibly against the United States. With the 2016 election fiasco, it could be reality.

Possibly, by laying his cards on the table like this, he might be able to force some action that would give him away. He needed to call and warn his operative to be on the lookout and watch his back.

As he finished his morning walk, Chicky picked up the newspaper from the front stoop and went into the house for his coffee. Telling himself he had a bit of time, he decided to drink his coffee, take his morning swim before making his call. They would need to formulate a plan. They had found so many spies, but this one was elusive.

The Keurig was already filled with water, so he inserted his pod and pressed down on the handle. With steaming cup in hand, he took the elixir of life into his bedroom and put on his swim trunks. Funny, he thought, they don't call them swim trunks any more.

Everyone in the house was still asleep but he knew they would be up shortly. He and his older children all had plans to take the boat out later for lunch in Forked River. It should be nice and quiet out on the bay today, with so many people leaving the island now that summer was over. In addition, there was little wind which would help keep the waves down, making for a smoother voyage.

There were a few decent restaurants out that way that could be accessed by boat. Dock hands came out and helped tie the boat to the pilings while the boaters got off onto the docks that jutted out into the water from the restaurant. The food was basically the same no matter where they went: burgers, fish sandwiches, salads and pizza. There were daily beer and drink specials. He preferred the restaurants around Washington, D.C. but those days were over.

He had informed his colleagues he would be retiring, sold the family home in Virginia and moved full time to Loveladies, New Jersey. He had hoped to wrap up his cases by year end. His children came to visit frequently, much to his dismay. He would prefer to be here by himself not having to deal with their pettiness. He knew all they wanted was his money and his property. He sighed; at least they will be gone after Labor Day and he could get on with his quiet life and completing his unfinished business hopefully by the end of the year.

With the jolt of caffeine in his old body, he felt energized enough for his morning swim up and down the lagoon. Exiting from the back door, he went to the dock, dove in and began his swim toward the bay. The water felt good this time of year, still warm for his creaky, old bones.

The movement and warmth loosened him up and he began to swim faster. Reaching the end of the lagoon by the Wilson house, he made his turn left to begin his swim down the opposite side. No one seemed to be out this morning, he mused, as he pulled himself through the water. He remembered this time of year as a parent, getting the kids off to school, missing the best weather and no crowds on the island. He certainly did not miss those days!

Rounding the other end of the lagoon for the final six hundred or so feet back to his dock, he started to plan the rest of his week in his head. Deep in thought, he didn't see or sense another person swimming directly behind him. As he began to pull himself up the ladder to his dock, strong hands pulled his body under the water. Struggling, he felt lines from the boat wrap around his hands, feet and body, making it difficult to rise up for air. He thrashed frantically, ramming his head against the hull of his boat, and then inhaling a fatal amount of water into his lungs.

To help conceal the body and make it look like an accident, the killer pushed Chicky under his boat. He then took the lines that were around the body and secured a few to the prop, to keep the body from popping out from underneath the hull.

The killer slowly made his way back to his home, swimming under the cover of the other homeowners' docks, boats and kayaks along the lagoon. Soon the noise of discovery would begin and there would be questions to answer.

About 15 minutes later, shouts were heard along the lagoon, the few neighbors who were still around came out on their docks to see what the commotion was all about. To their horror, they saw a body being pulled out of the water, limp and lifeless. Cries went out for an ambulance, the police, and paramedics to come help. One of the neighbors yelled that he was calling 911.

Sirens were soon followed by a throng of people onto to the street and back yard of the Haverford property. First responders tried desperately to revive the dead man as the family looked on in shock. Oxygen and CPR were applied, but failed. Finally, they called it, he was gone.

With the medical examiner on his way to formally pronounce him dead, the police began to question neighbors if they saw or heard anything unusual that morning. Since this was the last day of the holiday weekend, residents were busy packing up to return to their primary residences and work the next day. No information was available and no one had seen Chicky Haverford start or finish his swim that morning.

Of course, everyone knew him and had seen him swim in the lagoon many times, but not today. No, they really didn't know him well, he wasn't that friendly they would say, and they did not want to speak ill of the dead. The police got the picture though and had borne the brunt of many of his phone calls complaining of the neighbor's dog loose on his property, or someone knocking over his trash cans. He would berate the officers for not correcting these problems, saying the only thing they were good at was pulling over drivers who drove in the left hand lane on the boulevard.

The body was eventually bagged, tagged and removed, leaving the family alone in their realization that he was gone. After showing their disgust of the neighbors gawking into their private life, the family moved inside. They would need to make preparations for his funeral and burial.

Onlookers would say the family might be in shock; people on this particular lagoon might say they were already counting and spending his money.

Questions continued for the next few days. Of course, the family members were suspected of foul play knowing the worth of the deceased, but neither the police nor the medical examiner could find any evidence to suggest any of them was involved with his drowning. Neighbors who heard the initial shouting had gone outside and reported seeing the son start to kneel down on the dock and pull the father up from the water. The son had been dry before he knelt down. Once the father was out of the water, he was soaking wet. None of the family appeared to have been in the water and the women were quite dressed up and made up since they were planning on going for a nice, early lunch after Chicky was done with his swim.

Preliminary cause of death was accidental drowning; the authorities assumed he got tangled up in the lines under his boat, and being unable to get free of them, hit his head on the bottom of the boat and drowned. The investigation was stopped for lack of any evidence to the contrary.

Keslie Patch-Bohrod

CHAPTER 3

May 24, 2018 - Thursday

Miranda was so looking forward to this summer on Long Beach Island, on New Jersey's east coast. It had been a tough, cold, long winter with too much snow and too little sunlight. They had endured snow storm after snow storm in the early spring, barely digging out of one when another one dumped a foot or more of snow. She hated winter.

There had been several big projects at home that had kept her busy during the week, it seemed there was always something that needed to be repaired, replaced, revamped or thrown away. On the weekends, she and her husband Jack would visit their kids at college, alternating between the two. Kevin and Erica always wanted her to put out a big spread for their friends at the football tailgates. She really hadn't minded all the preparation and packing of the car, because it meant they would want to spend time with her and Jack.

Then the holidays came; shopping, entertaining and family for Thanksgiving, Christmas and New Year's Day. The kids were home for about month with piles of laundry and requests for special meals.

It seemed like the holidays were just over when it was Spring Break and they were back home doing it all over again. They usually tried to open the house at the shore early if it looked like the weather would cooperate but with all the snow; they didn't get the chance this year.

In addition, she and Jack were looking to buy an apartment building as an investment. This required many visits to the site, meetings with the real estate agents and of course meetings with their bank regarding financing options. The present owner wasn't interested in closing right away.

They were hoping for some time in September or October when most of the existing tenant leases would expire.

Miranda was looking forward to this. Her job would be property manager; she had even studied and passed the exam for a New Jersey real estate license. Knowing the ins and outs of contracts, rental and sales agreements would be very beneficial. It had been just one more thing on her very long to do list she was able to tick off. Come hell or high water, she was going to have a quiet, relaxing summer because in September, her life would be extremely busy with this new venture, plus there were a number of trips planned in the fall.

The kids were finally finished with their college exams and it was up to Miranda to drive to their schools and help load up cars with the accumulation of stuff from the year. Neither one of them could fit everything in one car. Jack, of course, was busy working during the week, so it was up to her to get them packed up and back home. They never really bothered unloading their cars since most of the possessions would just go back to school in a few months. The winter clothes had been switched out at home during spring break for spring and summer attire and would go directly to the shore. Miranda's car would be unloaded since it was the biggest and generally carried the furniture items like the TV, refrigerator, microwave and bookshelves. Now all they had to do was decide what else they needed to get ready to begin their summer jobs at the shore. The kids enjoyed their jobs, co-workers and the money they made but not the long, hot hours they put in.

It was always hectic trying to get everything done and the cars loaded. The thought of just relaxing by the pool doing nothing was the incentive that enticed everyone to do their part. They rushed around the house, gathering clothes, shoes, bathing suits, toiletries and anything they thought they would need for the summer at the shore.

Getting an early start was imperative to beat the holiday traffic. With predicted warm sunny weather, everyone would want to spend time at the beach. There were many shore points along the Garden State Parkway, some of the more popular being Asbury Park, Point Pleasant, Margate, Ocean City , Sandy Hook, and Cape May to the south just to name a few. Traffic would begin to reduce the further south one traveled.

Food was shoved into plastic grocery bags, perishables were thrown into a big Igloo cooler just in case they were caught in traffic longer than expected. They bumped into each other as they rushed out the door to load their cars.

The dog began to get nervous, sensing their anxiety trying to get everything done and also fearing he wouldn't be going with them. Each stopped to pat him on the head and assured him he was going along too. Only after they pulled down his leash from the shelf and gathered his food cans and bag, did he relax and feel more at ease with the bustle going on around him.

It was the same at the beginning of each summer. School let out, mad rush to get out of town and begin summer vacation. The draw to the shore was incredible. Was it the peace and serenity, the togetherness as a family, the ocean and salt air, or the great accumulated memories of years past?

"Come on everyone, we have to get on the road early to beat all the traffic for the Memorial Day holiday weekend. You know what it will be like trying to get on the island if we wait until tonight or tomorrow morning. It will take four to five hours rather than two." Miranda was not looking forward to the drive, no matter how many hours it took. Leaving on a Thursday morning was the best time to head out. It seemed in New Jersey, traffic was always an issue, no matter the time of day or route taken. In addition, New Jersey drivers could be ruthless and reckless especially on the Garden State Parkway.

"Mom, Kevin and I are taking our own cars, too. There is no way I am going to be stuck borrowing your car all summer long. Besides, I have shopping to do. I have to get a new bikini at Ron Jon's before all the good ones are sold out," said Erica, her twenty-one year old daughter.

"That's fine, but both of you are paying for your own gas. Once we get to the house, you will have to help unload all the food, clothing and supplies we need to get this summer started. Then you can go see Antonio about your summer work schedules."

Miranda was anxious to get the kids back to work so she could settle down and get her work done- cleaning the house after being shut up all winter long. She had called their plumber the prior week to turn on the water, gas and electric and make sure everything was ship shape. The air conditioner needed to be serviced and the water heater checked to make sure it was in working order too. They didn't need the hassle of a broken dishwasher or any other appliance. If anything did not work over the weekend, no tradesman would come out or they would charge an exorbitant fee.

"We have had a nasty winter and I am looking forward to some peace and quiet this summer, getting my garden started and reading as many books as possible. The weather is supposed to be hot and sunny and we will be able to hang around the pool, relax and start to work on our tans. Hopefully, Dad can finish work early enough today to join us for cocktails by the pool."

Miranda was worried that Jack might not get out of the office. The stock market was tanking because the President of the United States was making disparaging comments about a certain company. Many of Jack's clients, who held stock in this company, were starting to panic as the stock market plummeted and he would be expected to do a lot of hand holding until things quieted down. Jack's company, Craig Wealth Management, was well known in the state as one of the more prosperous investment firms. His team of stock analysts could perform miracles but not when the President targeted one company in particular. The overall effect on the market was frightening. At least Jack could handle business over the phone, which not being the best option, was at least an option that might allow him to come to the shore to be with his family.

Miranda and the kids finished packing up their respective cars. By the time she got the dog, Maynard, a six year old Weimaraner mix, in the back seat, the kids were gone like a puff of smoke before she could tell them to drive carefully. She worried about them with all the crazy drivers out there.

Family was the most important thing for Miranda. She loved spending time with them, but with the kids and Jack working so much it would be difficult this summer. She would have to plan special meals and make the best of what time they had together.

She had worked most of her adult life; the longest position had been with an insurance company as an investigator, primarily on Workers' Compensation claims. This had been her favorite job. It had provided her with the freedom to come and go as she pleased as long as she 'got the goods' on the claimants who were trying to defraud the system.

It wasn't a hard job; it just required cunning beyond that of the claimant. Most weren't that smart. They never suspected that mother with a diaper bag and baby carriage had been videotaping them chopping down a tree in the backyard or playing baseball with their kids when they were supposed to be seriously injured. Some even had the audacity to work, collecting wages under the table, while collecting workers' compensation checks. Big no no. Second degree felony.

The report would be written, submitting the photographs and video and even statements from the unwitting employers. Catching someone doing something wrong had always thrilled Miranda. She took great pleasure when these criminals were prosecuted.

Some of the cases had gotten a bit dicey, one especially. She had been spotted in her car watching a claimant's house. She wasn't a small woman and she certainly wasn't some big body builder. Having taken a number of courses that taught personal protection at the insistence of her husband, she had been able to take down a very abusive man who also had a previous record of criminal assault and drug dealing.

She had been watching him for over a week, taking pictures of him moving what looked like heavy boxes from his garage into this wife's minivan. He had been a construction worker who supposedly hurt his back on a work site. His attorney had insisted the insurance company refer him to a particular doctor for his medical care. This doctor was known to exaggerate an injury so the claimant could get a bigger settlement. It was Miranda's job to prove otherwise. Unfortunately, Miranda had gotten distracted when a phone call came in from her boss.

By the time she noticed the man charging at her car, she had little time to react. He had opened her door and pulled her forcefully from the car. Being in fear of her life, she wasn't afraid to use self-defense moves that would cause severe injury; she only had a minute to stop him.

As he pulled her toward him, she continued the forward momentum even faster than he imagined she would. First, her right thumb went into his eye socket and dug deep. He shouted in pain, releasing her left arm. Immediately, she kneed him in the groin with enough force that surely would cause him to bend over with both of his hands going to his crotch. Then, she drove her heal onto the top of his foot, hoping for a few broken bones which would make walking impossible. Finally, she clasped her hands together and brought them down on the base of his neck where she could see one of the bones of the cervical spine sticking out.

Thinking that should about do it, she returned to her car and called the police and her office. When the police arrived, she explained who she was, why she was there and what she suspected. When the police took a look inside of the boxes he was loading into the van, they found they were filled with cocaine. Not only was she sending this guy to the hospital, she was also sending him back to prison on a number of different counts.

But that all ended when she gave birth to Kevin. Not only did she not want to go back to work right away, but her company had suffered a number of serious catastrophic losses. Another insurance company took them over and her position was downsized.

The generous severance package had been nice and Jack immediately invested it for her. It had grown exponentially over the years and continued to generate dividends. They really didn't need her to work but she missed the interaction with co-workers and the challenges of a job. She had had a number of other positions over the years lasting a year or two at a time. But for whatever reason, the jobs ended. So she devoted herself to her family and home. And summer was all about taking care of her family and enjoying what time they had together on glorious LBI.

Miranda scolded herself for letting her mind wander while she was behind the wheel. She needed to pay attention as cars and trucks were coming onto the roadway or changing lanes. The drive to Long Beach Island was always a pain and could be dangerous. Route 287 and the Garden State Parkway in New Jersey could be bumper to bumper at a moment's notice. The ninety mile trek today would give Miranda the time to mentally wind down, if the traffic would only cooperate.

As only a dog owner would understand, Miranda started talking to Maynard, mainly because no one else was in the car. "I hope we have a good summer this year. When everyone is gone and doing their own thing, all I want to do is sit alone, in silence. I can't wait to sit by the pool and hear the leaves rustling from the neighbor's tree. I wish I knew what kind of tree it is; I'd plant one in our backyard. Maynard, you know how it is; we go to Loveladies because we want the lack of stimulation- to withdraw from society, from contact with others. Life is so different in Loveladies, it is quiet and serene. I am sure you feel the same way, you seem to really enjoy sitting on the deck looking out at the lagoon watching for ducks or egrets, barking at boaters, or swimmers in the water. It is just a peaceful, boring world there." Of course Maynard did not respond, he was already sound asleep on the back seat of her Ford Explorer.

The drive was surprisingly uneventful. There was only a little traffic on the highways and thankfully no accidents that would cause a major delay. Miranda spotted the highway sign for Exit 63 Route 72, East for Long Beach Island and Manahawkin and West for Pemberton. She moved her car into the right lane and slowed as she took the exit ramp. She took the right curving lane that would put her on Route 72 East.

She couldn't help but remember what Jack would always tell her each time they took this exit.

"You can't imagine what it used to be like. None of this was here", he would say. "No Costco or Target, no big car dealerships, no big shopping centers surrounding the Lowes or the Home Depot. There used to be a drive-in movie theater where the Kmart used to be. Some of the old time marinas were still there, but now the old was being torn down and the new and improved was going up."

She had never seen this area in its old state and found it hard to comprehend. She tried to imagine what it looked like back in the 1960s and 1970s; the roadway was probably lined with only trees and pines. This area was part of the Pine Barrens of New Jersey, and home of the Jersey Devil which was a crazy creature now the mascot of the New Jersey Devil's hockey team. Who knew if the Devil actually existed, some claimed to have seen something in the swamps, but it was never photographed, much like the Loch Ness monster.

The thought of not having the luxury of all the stores and companies made Miranda wonder what their life would have been like. Whites Grocery Store in Barnegat Light and Ocean Market in Ship Bottom had been around for decades, providing only the basics and charging high prices for the convenience.

The Craig's would surely be eating very plain meals or she would have had to bring all the food and necessities from home. What a pain that would have been.

Thankfully, that wasn't the case anymore, and she could find almost any food item she wanted at the ShopRite or Costco off the island. There was only one full sized grocery store on the island and it took twice as long to get there so she just went off the island where there were many options.

The bridge that crossed from the mainland to the island was undergoing major repair and expansion. A second bridge was being built right next to it and the original would be redone. Once completed, in the event of a hurricane, all four lanes on both bridges would become outgoing to facilitate a swift evacuation off the island. Miranda shook her head and wondered what genius devised that plan. She guessed they never witnessed New Jersey drivers vying for one entrance ramp onto the interstate. Not a pretty sight! In the event of a hurricane even approaching the East Coast, Miranda pledged to be the first off the island before any merging would take place.

As she crossed the bridge, she looked to the North and saw a few boats on the Bay of Manahawkin enjoying the beautiful day. Glancing to the South, she was able to see the Atlantic City skyline in the distance and wondered if she and Jack might be able to get away this summer for some Blackjack, dinner and a show. It was only about 45 minutes to an hour away, and the casinos had some great restaurants. Maybe she and Jack could check the calendar and scheduled shows this weekend and see when they might have a date night.

Miranda's phone rang as she was getting onto the island. It was her summer friend, Liz Goldberg, who lived directly across the lagoon from the Craig's. In Loveladies, the section of Long Beach Island where they lived, had a series of lagoons that had been dredged back in the early 1950s with houses built along the edges of the water. It made for a blissful and picturesque location.

"Miranda, its Liz. I figured you were on your way to the shore and I knew I had to reach you before you got here. I've been meaning to call you all year, since last Labor Day weekend, but with everything that has been going on with us I never got around to it. I know I should have kept you in the loop but I am sure you will eventually forgive me." Miranda knew she wouldn't get a word in so she just kept driving and waited for Liz to finish her ramblings.

"Anyway, you are just going to die when I tell you the gossip from last Labor Day. I know you and Jack had to leave early to help one of the kids move back into their college dorm. But damn, it was no sooner I see you guys pull out, that the police show up next door at the Haverford's. Apparently, old man Haverford had gone out to take his daily morning swim in the lagoon. You know how you always say you see him out there doing his slow Australian crawl up and down the lagoon. Well, his family got worried when he didn't come in for breakfast. The son went out to check on him and found him wedged under his boat tangled up in line. The police think he hit his head on the back of his boat and got caught up in the lines that were hanging off there and somehow got stuck under the boat. No one heard a thing. A few neighbors were still here on the lagoon, but they all said they were inside all morning and hadn't seen him out for his swim. Miranda, you know he was older than dirt. I'm surprised he could even tread water, let alone do laps in the lagoon. The police don't suspect foul play; although, I don't think they closed the case yet. An autopsy was performed at the request of the family, but of course we have no idea about the results. He wasn't a friendly man, and most the neighbors did not like him. He had a problem with us because of our dog getting into his yard a couple of times. Remember when we were building our house last year and the run-ins we would have? Jesus, we had run-ins on the other side too with Alek! Is it us or is it them?"

Miranda couldn't believe what Liz was telling her and the fact that she had not heard about his death last fall. Chicky Haverford wasn't a nice man, but he didn't deserve to die that way. Or did he? Although Miranda did have secret fantasies about him drowning in the lagoon and her running into the house so she wouldn't have to save him.

Liz said, "Miranda, that's not all. His kids inherited the property and have razed the house. This next tidbit is going to kill you, I know how much you loved it; they cut down the tree."

Miranda almost drove off the road. That tree was special. She had even asked a landscaper at one point years ago about that tree and the prospects of planting one on their property. There really wasn't enough space the way their house, shed and pool were laid out. She knew she was being ridiculous, but the sound it made when a breeze came down the lagoon was sheer bliss. To her, it symbolized the quiet solitude of Loveladies. It would never be the same in Loveladies without that tree. Miranda got a sick feeling in her stomach and wondered if this was foreboding of other bad things to come?

Miranda finally got to the house and pulled onto the rocks in the front yard. Most of the houses on the island had river rock instead of grass to conserve water and reduce the upkeep required. Compared to the other houses on the street, their home reminded her of a double wide trailer. But its outward appearance was deceiving. The house was shaped like the letter 'F' and was really much larger than it appeared from the front or back. They were slowly but surely making improvements to the old house, such as redoing the kitchen and two bathrooms with updated fixtures and appliances. It was more important for them to be with family and friends than have an impressive, expensive house.

Of course, the kids were already there and came running out to tell Miranda about the Haverford house. The view from the backyard was depressing- no house and no tree. Liz saw Miranda on the dock and came out.

"Miranda, Richard and I want you and Jack to come to dinner some night over the weekend. Let me know what night is best. I am going to check with some of the other neighbors to see if I can find out any more about Chicky's death and what his kids plan to do."

"How about we come over Saturday night?" Miranda said after gauging how much work she had to do to get the house cleaned and when she thought Jack would be down. "We will bring the wine and an appetizer, anything else you need?"

"No that sounds good, I think ShopRite has lobsters on sale, so I will run out there Saturday morning at the crack of dawn and beat all the Shoe bee's and renters coming onto the island. You know what traffic is like on a Saturday morning. If I don't get out there early, it will take me an hour or more to get back. Why don't you come over about six-thirty?"

With the plans all worked out, Miranda rounded up the kids to unload the cars. With everyone helping, it only took about a half an hour. She sent them off to Antonio's to get their work schedules.

All Miranda could think about was that tree. It had been in the far corner of the property by the lagoon. The builder could have worked around it. What on Earth possessed them to cut it down?

Keslie Patch-Bohrod

CHAPTER 4

May 25 & 26, 2018 - Friday and Saturday of Memorial Day weekend

Miranda worked like a house on fire all day Friday, cleaning the bathrooms, washing the bedding, mopping the floors and checking that the kitchen had everything she needed for the summer. She opened all the windows to air out the musty smell that develops when a house is closed up for so long. The kids had left early for their first day back at work and they wouldn't be home until late tonight. This year they told her they would go out to dinner and drinks with their co-workers and take the LBI shuttle home when the bars closed down. They would take the shuttle to work in the morning and drive their cars home the next day. That way they wouldn't drink and drive and Miranda wouldn't have to come pick them up late at night.

Jack had called and said he wouldn't be able to get away from the office because of scheduled client meetings. He promised he would leave right after a business lunch date on Saturday. So, it would be a nice quiet evening home alone with her book, TV and dog.

The next day, Miranda decided to make some kind of dip for the appetizer that night. She went to Cassidy's fish market in Barnegat Light and purchased some bunker to put in their crab trap. It was early in the season and she wasn't sure she would catch anything, but she would give it a try.

Taking the large red crab trap from the shed, she went over to their dock and secured the piece of fish inside and lowered the trap into the lagoon, securing the rope to the wooden piling. She would check it frequently so see if she caught anything. Crabs couldn't be left in the trap for long, if there were more than one, they had a tendency to fight and rip the claws off each other.

Later that afternoon, she went out again to check the trap. *I must be livin' right*, she said to herself as she counted the number of crabs in the trap. Two would have to go back because they were too small, the other three were keepers. She shook the trap to loosen the crabs into separate buckets of water; if she didn't separate them they would tear each other apart. Thinking how ironic that was, especially when she was just going to throw them into a big pot of boiling water.

She set a large kettle on the stove filled with water and dumped in a huge amount of Old Bay seasoning. When the water was boiling, she brought the crabs in and put them into the water to cook for about twelve minutes. The smell of the Old Bay was wonderful as it permeated the house.

After the cooked crab cooled, she picked out as much of the meat she could and added it to cream cheese, chopped artichoke hearts, garlic, parmesan cheese, spinach and a number of fresh herbs. She really didn't have a recipe, but with those ingredients how could it be bad.

Jack made it to the house minutes before they had to leave to go to Liz and Richard's on Saturday evening. Of course, leaving on Saturday afternoon had been a nightmare for Jack; it was bumper to bumper all the way. He was in a "mood" and Miranda knew they had to get to their neighbors and put a glass of wine in his hand before his mood turned even uglier. Usually, he would like to get to the house and immediately go to the beach for a swim in the ocean, saying that it had magical powers of washing away all the stress of the world. Tonight, he would just have to rely on the Amizetta cabernet that she had pulled out of the wine refrigerator.

They decided to walk over knowing they would have many bottles of wine that night. It was only a five minute walk and this would give Jack a few more minutes to decompress from the week at work. They would have time tomorrow to catch up with each other's day and week after sleeping in and enjoying a quiet morning.

Liz was chomping at the bit and almost attacked them as they came to the door. She couldn't wait to talk to the two of them about what happened to Chicky. She ushered them in, took the wine and gave it to Richard to open and popped the crab dip appetizer

Miranda made in the toaster oven to keep it warm while they got everything situated.

"I hope you like Lobster Newberg" said Liz, "I found what looked like a good recipe in a Martha Stewart cookbook. Boiled or steamed lobsters seemed like a truly boring dinner to kick start the summer. Thankfully, I was able to buy a bunch of lobsters at ShopRite for five dollars and ninety-nine cents a pound; you know how they have their lobster sales a couple times during the summer. Plus, this recipe let me get everything together and put in the oven right when you were set to arrive. It will bake for twenty-five minutes, which is just long enough for us to chat and have appetizers."

As they sat outside in the Goldberg's screened-in porch, Jack could sense that something was up. Looking at Liz and Richard, he said, "OK, what have I missed? Why do you and Richard have this goofy look on your face?"

"I guess Miranda didn't have time to tell you the news or she was waiting for us to tell you all the details we know up to this point" said Liz. "So, if everyone has their wine, and the 'appies' are on the table, I will share what I have found out."

"As I told Miranda Thursday, Chicky Haverford was found dead under his boat last Labor Day Weekend. He had gone out for his swim and was late coming back. His son found him and called the police. They have ruled it an accident but it just seems weird. Even though he was old, he was a very good swimmer. There was no evidence of a stroke or heart attack either."

"Maybe I'm reverting back to my insurance investigation days, but you are right. It does seem weird," admitted Miranda. "With all the people around here, even at the end of the summer, you would think someone would have heard or seen something. Well, at least I think Maynard or I would have heard or seen something. It makes me think that someone sneaked up on him and killed him. That would be a really clever way of killing someone don't you think? All they have to do is slink back into the water and swim out to the bay to an awaiting boat."

"Oh, my god, Miranda, here you go again with these crazy theories!" Obviously, Jack hadn't had enough wine to smooth out his irritation. "Not only that, but you are always watching the neighbors, checking to see what cars are on the street, doing your Gladys routine."

Liz's and Richard's eyebrows went up and in unison as they said, "Who is Gladys?"

"You remember her, she was the nosy neighbor in the old TV show *Bewitched"* explained Jack. *"*Gladys Kravitz was always watching Samantha Steven's house, who was the witch. She would see the house disappear and yell to her husband Abner to come look. By the time he would get to the window, the house would reappear. Gladys always looked like a kook. Miranda's obsession and why I gave her the nickname all started when we were broken into."

Miranda told Liz and Richard the story of when they had a home invasion in their home up North. After that, Miranda became vigilant about the comings and goings around her. She took notice of delivery vans, mail carriers, the kids walking home from school down their street. She knew when the other neighbors changed landscapers or had furniture delivered.

The break-in had really scared her. They had been home this particular Friday night about fifteen years ago. Jack had to work Saturday so they would go the shore Saturday afternoon.

The kids being small had fallen asleep across the foot of their bed while watching the Discovery Channel. Jack too, was sound asleep. Miranda was still awake, trying to decide if she wanted to go to sleep or find something else to watch. It was only 10:00 p.m. She decided she would search through the online channel guide before arming the house alarm, turning on the outside lights and putting the kids into their beds.

She was scrolling the listings, when she heard a huge crash. Her initial thought was it sounded like one of their bookcases in the office fell over. But that couldn't be. Then she heard another crash. Jumping out of bed she quickly ran to the landing at the top of the stairs. All the air rushed out of her lungs as she saw the bouncing pin light ascending the stairs in front of her. She turned and tried to shout, "Jack, someone is in the house!"

Seconds later Jack was beside her, they heard another crash and the two rushed down the stairs in the dark. Jack turned on the foyer light and they looked around. Nothing seemed out of place. As they started looking in other rooms, Jack shouted, "Miranda, come into the office; I found something." Miranda rushed over to Jack and saw the entire front door knob and lockset on the floor. They turned on outside lights, opened the front door and looked around. Seeing nothing, Jack instructed Miranda to call 911.

Miranda, having picked up the land line called out, "There's no dial tone; they must have cut the phone lines! Where is your cell?"

About five minutes after placing the call, the town's police chief and several officers arrived. They told the Craigs there had been a rash of break-ins in the area and that they were lucky they scared them away. Their MO was one man would break in the front door while the second man cut the phone lines. The first would run upstairs and grab cash, jewelry and anything of value, while the second ran to the basement and cut the security system wires.

As Chief Stover relayed this information to Jack and Miranda, he received another call that a house had just been broken into three streets up from the Craigs, possibly the same men who had broken into their home. One of the officers left to attend to those homeowners, while the chief and the remaining officers helped Jack board up the front door. All the while, unbelievably, Kevin and Erica slept through the whole ordeal.

Needless to say, the Craigs, especially Miranda, began to take their security more seriously. Their alarm was always set and they had an electrician install a number of motion detection outdoor lights that would come on if someone or something was nearby. Jack often joked about Miranda's vigilance calling her Gladys.

Keeping an eye out in Loveladies was critical too. Their shore house had been burgled one year, with TV's and computers being the only things of value in the house to take. Of course, no one was caught. There was very little activity on the island, especially at their end, before the summer season started. Loveladies was part of Long Beach Township which had a separate police force from the other little towns. Officers had to travel some ten to fifteen miles from the station to Loveladies. Even if men were seen going into a house, it might be assumed they were plumbers or electricians given a key to get the house ready for the season or to make a repair. Of course, this was a number of years ago and people had yet to install outdoor cameras on their property.

"Oh my god you guys, I can't believe that happened to you!" Liz said as she pulled their dinner out of the oven and placed it on the table. "Now I can understand why you would be so paranoid about what goes on. With the kids working crazy hours or going out with their friends and Jack coming down only on the weekends, you are left alone most of the time. Do you ever get frightened?"

"Sure, it can get creepy down here at night especially during the week when there aren't too many people down here. Those winter or spring weekends when I would come down here by myself when Jack was out of town were scary." Miranda started to explain, "But during the summer, there are generally enough people in their homes on our street or on the lagoon that I feel safe. The break-in was due to our stupidity. We left a key in the outdoor shower and that's how they got in. This was a tradition of sorts down here for years. Almost everyone has an outdoor shower area either attached to the house or separate; it's great for when you come back from the beach all sandy. You shower outside and don't leave half of the beach on your floors. These little rooms were great for leaving a key or some item for someone to pick up. It was just so convenient to leave a key in the shower so if you needed work done, the plumber or whoever could get into your house. They would return it when they were finished with the work. Well, someone took advantage of our trustworthiness and used our key to steal from us. They even broke the key off in the door. We had to get all new locks, keys and door knobs. The break-ins were the reason we got a big dog, so I am not going to let that bother me. He is our security alarm. You know how crazy he gets when someone comes to the door, a boat is coming down the lagoon or kids are out paddle boarding or kayaking, he barks his head off. "

"No matter what happened down here I don't think I would ever not want to be here. You don't think anything can happen because it so boring here. The worst things that happen during the season are thefts at the construction sites and maybe kids stealing stuff from unlocked cars. Or heaven forbid, someone puts a bag of dog poop in your trash can, not in one of the garbage bags. Then when the garbage collectors come, they refuse to take it, either by throwing it on the street or putting it back in your trash can."

"The police department is responsive and over the years has become more proactive in protecting the community. If your house will be vacant for a period of time, you submit a form and they will keep a closer watch over your property. I remember last Spring Break, Kevin arrived at the house before me. When I got here Kevin was showing his driver's license to an officer. I had forgotten to call the town and inform them we would be coming for that week. Poor Kevin, you should have seen the look on his face when I pulled in."

Liz responded, "Yes, I saw that on the town website and I will do that for next winter. And you are right; you just don't think anything will happen here. That was one reason we picked Loveladies to build our house. The other reason was that it seemed the neighbors pretty much keep to themselves. It is so relaxing and quiet. When you are just sitting out on the deck by the pool in the sun, the only thing that goes on is maybe a boat or swimmer going up the lagoon."

Miranda agreed. "We read, listen to light music and sink into that delicious boredom that is Loveladies. Your senses are awakened by the smell of the flowers and herbs or someone grilling, the ha-ha-ha sound of the seagulls, water lapping against the bulkhead, or the warmth of the sunshine on your skin. We don't want to move, we don't want to go out. The farthest we will travel is a few streets, like to your house! We have friends in Normandy Beach and Ortley that invite us all the time to come see them which would require us to leave the island, get on the parkway and travel about thirty minutes. We won't do it and they hate us for it. Only someone that lives here understands the feeling of not wanting to find something to do. We have to force ourselves to get work done. Jack has the eleven o'clock rule. We walk, bike, do chores until eleven then…whatever. But of course, that's only when he is here. When I'm alone, I tend to be doing chores almost all day and night.

Liz hesitantly began, "Miranda, I hate to tell you this, but late this afternoon I heard from our builder that Chicky Haverford's kids just got the go ahead with their construction project next door. They are building a big house, deck, pool and landscaping and word has it, the wife is a real task master ordering it done before Labor Day.

With them being across the lagoon from you, you will hear the non-stop construction from seven in the morning until six o'clock every day. Say goodbye to your quiet summer."

CHAPTER 5

May 27 - Sunday

The previous two days had been very slow at the deli leading Antonio to believe not many people had come to the island for the holiday or were doing all the cooking themselves. Both kids were able to get the day off, but had to be on call if a delivery order came in. Kevin and Erica didn't have a problem with this because it was the best way to make a bunch of money in a short amount of time. One time last year, Kevin delivered a box of sandwiches to a house on the beach in Loveladies and received not only the twenty dollar delivery fee but a hefty one hundred dollar tip. There was a crazy amount of money on this island and thankfully, some of the people had a soft spot for nice kids.

So Jack took the kids out on the boat for the morning, staying close around the Bay in case Antonio called with a delivery time. They would return for lunch, and then the plan was to relax around the pool for the remainder of the day. These days would be few and far between. The temperature was in the mid-seventies, sunny with a light, fragrant breeze off the ocean. The location of the wind was critical to a nice day. If the wind came off the bay, you could count on green headed flies delivering huge, painful welts that would itch ferociously.

Miranda thought about the day ahead and decided on a plan for lunch to set the mood for the rest of the day. She filled a large pot with cold water, added a generous pinch of salt and set it on the stove. She turned the heat on high and began to cut and clean two large bunches of broccoli rabe. Since everyone would be home today for lunch, she thought she would make some special sandwiches.

The chicken breasts were seasoned with salt and pepper, which she would grill later, closer to lunch time. As the water began to bubble on their quick boil burner, Miranda put the broccoli rabe in to blanch for about 5 minutes. In the meantime, she added chopped garlic, red pepper flakes, seasoned salt and pepper to extra virgin olive oil in a sauté pan, cooking just long enough to become fragrant.

The blanched vegetable was strained then rinsed in cold water before adding to the oil mixture. As the broccoli rabe reduced in size dramatically, she added half a can of chicken broth and half a cup of white wine. She would let this simmer until tender about twenty minutes. Next, to prepare the real flavor for the sandwich she took a half of a large jar of sun dried tomatoes in olive oil and herbs, and half a jar of Kirkland pesto, she blended the two in her Cuisinart until smooth.

It was getting close to noon, so Miranda took the chicken and grilled it outside on their Weber. She warmed the ciabatta bread until crispy and sliced it lengthwise. The sun-dried tomato pesto was slathered on the bottom piece of bread; the grilled chicken was put on top of that. The broccoli rabe nestled on the chicken and then layers of freshly sliced buffalo mozzarella. The open faced sandwiches were put on cookie sheets and placed in the oven until the cheese began to melt. The crispy top of the bread went on last. She could almost taste them as she plated the sandwiches, serving with it a cool three bean salad and a chilled bottle of Guy Allion Sauvignon Blanc 2016. This was a nice, crisp, inexpensive white wine, perfect for a Loveladies lunch on the deck.

Jack and the kids docked their twenty-five foot Boston Whaler and joined her at the outdoor table, marveling at the wonderful lunch she had prepared for them. She knew she spoiled them, but there was nothing better in this world for her than being with her family, eating wonderful food, drinking good wine, and enjoying the Loveladies lifestyle.

They spent the remainder of the afternoon lounging by the pool. The kids humored her and put on her favorite Pandora radio station- Pink Martini. The light, jazzy sounds were perfect for the day. Jack had thoughtfully turned on the heater so they could swim in the pool. It wouldn't be until mid-July that the summer high temperatures would sufficiently heat it.

They decided a simple dinner of grilled shrimp and zucchini with yellow rice would end the day nicely. The kids had been lucky, or not and hadn't received any calls for deliveries. They would work a long shift tomorrow after a full day of rest.

Miranda and Jack didn't have any plans for Memorial Day other than working on the garden and trimming down the Butterfly bushes in the front planting beds. Every year, they cut them down and by the end of the summer they would be over nine feet tall. They would attract a ton of Monarch butterflies and at times it could be dangerous entering the house from the front door. The butterflies would bombard from all directions, and then flit away. Of course, they were harmless, but it was a bit disconcerting nevertheless having all these flying objects darting around your face.

Jack would return to work on Tuesday morning and Miranda would go about the everyday chores of a housewife. The week would crawl by, with the kids coming home about seven at night, exhausted and hungry. She would make them something healthy to eat, because she knew they were picking at deli foods all day long.

One thing was for certain, Chicky's death didn't feel right. She needed more information on how he died and why. If it was natural, she would have to make sure Jack took care to bring in all loose lines from the outside of his boat so no swimmers could accidentally get caught up in them. If it was not a natural death, then she had to keep a close eye on the lagoon.

Keslie Patch-Bohrod

CHAPTER 6

June 1 - Friday

Up at six with the sun to feed Maynard, Miranda decided to make a trip off the island and do some shopping at Target and Costco, after she looked in the refrigerator and saw it was almost empty. Did the kids get up in the middle of night and eat it all? Jack would be coming down tomorrow so she would need to stock up on his favorites. She thought about starting a list, but decided it might just be easier to go down each aisle and start filling her cart.

When the kids got up, the first thing they asked was the standard, "What's for dinner?"

Usually she joked and said, "Dirt!"

Thankfully, Miranda had already thought that far ahead and had checked she had the ingredients available, "Chicken sausage, escarole, white cannellini beans, pasta with a white wine and garlic sauce, does that sound good?" Of course it was it was one of their many favorite meals.

She made them some scrambled eggs and whole grain toast for breakfast, letting them make their own coffee. They were like a pair of zombies in the morning, eyes half open, stumbling around. It was hard for them to work all summer, but she and Jack had agreed that it was good for their character to develop a strong work ethic and earn their own spending money for the school year. Most of their college friends also worked during the summer so it wasn't like they were asked to do something outrageous. They themselves had been the ones to pick where they worked. If they didn't like working there, they could always find other employment on the island. But to Jack and Miranda's amazement, each year they returned to Antonio's.

Once they were fed, dressed and out the door, Miranda checked the clock above the stove. It was approaching nine, so she quickly let Maynard outside for a bit while she got dressed and brushed her teeth.

It would take about thirty to forty minutes to get to Target, depending on the Friday morning island traffic. The slow speed limits and traffic lights really added to the overall drudgery of this chore. With grown, hungry kids, a husband with particular food tastes and a nonstop stream of company, she would have to make this trip two and maybe even three times a week.

She really didn't mind grocery shopping mainly because she enjoyed eating and cooking. It was the other idiots in the store that got to her. Emily Post would have a field day with the rudeness of people. Weekends were worse. No one understood shopping cart etiquette. It was just like driving a car, you stayed to the right of the aisle, allowed others to pass and kept moving. By no means make a sudden stop in front of another person with a shopping cart; otherwise the cart would take out the back of your ankles. Do not shop with the entire family! Their input was not needed nor did they need to clog up the aisle preventing someone from getting something from the shelf. Kids should be left at home. Husbands should be left at home. They didn't know what they were doing and had a tendency to walk down the middle of the aisle oblivious to all those around them. They dilly dallied.

And then there were the snacking stations at Costco. Employees staked a place at the end of an aisle and prepared samples of sausage, cheese, frozen pizza and the like. Shoppers crowded around waiting for the hot item to be put in the little paper cups. They pushed and shoved to be the first making it so hard to get around them.

Miranda could feel her blood pressure rise as she thought about getting this chore done. She finally made it to Target and ran in to collect a few items. Thank god they installed those self-serve checkout kiosks which moved things along. Yes, they took jobs away from people, but some of the clerks were so darn slow. It was best to give people the option.

She probably should get gas while at Costco but the line was very long and she was running low on patience. Heaven help her, it was barely ten in the morning. All she wanted to do was get back home and enjoy the day. She knew the construction would begin soon and wanted a quiet day to sit outside and maybe plant some seeds in her garden.

The doors were just opening up at Costco, so Miranda grabbed a cart from the corral and hustled inside. She took off at a quick pace hoping she could get in and get out without killing any one. Before she entered the store, she noticed a number of plants in the outer room where the shopping carts were stored at night. Luck would have it, tomato plants, fresh herbs, cucumber and peppers. She might need two carts! She took all she thought she could plant right away, saving lots of room in the cart for the rest of the food items she would need to buy. Stopping in the cold produce room, she threw lettuce, cucumbers, peppers, mushrooms, spinach, blackberries, and blueberries in the cart. Next, tomatoes, baguette, steaks, chicken breast, ribs, wild salmon, frozen shrimp, cheese, yogurt, skim milk, pita chips, dried herbs, season salt, pepper, flour, sugar, bouillon, canned San Marzano tomatoes, olive oil, and finally some cereal for the kids for when they were in a hurry in the morning. No one was in the checkout line yet, so she unloaded her cart and pulled out the credit card to pay for everything. Oh boy, this was a big bill! She couldn't remember the last time she got through her shopping this quickly.

She turned onto Route 72 East to head back to the island and was dismayed to see the long line of cars stretching out as far as the eye could see. The weather report promised upper seventies and sunny all weekend. With what she was seeing now, Miranda knew the island would be packed with owners and renters. That, at least, would hopefully translate into great tips for the kids.

It took over an hour to get back home. She had the air conditioning on full blast to help keep the car cool. Thankfully she had the presence of mind to keep the big cooler in the back of the Explorer and had loaded it with the perishable items.

It was after eleven thirty when she pulled onto their property. She rushed inside to feed Maynard his lunch- yes they fed him three times a day. It had started when he was a puppy and they never changed it. Why shouldn't he eat his meals about the same time they did?

By the time she had all the meat, chicken and fish separated into portions and put in Ziploc bags, the fruit cleaned and put into their own containers it was already one thirty. The plants had been unloaded and placed by the garden. Almost the entire day shot just buying groceries; she would have to start dinner soon!

Screw it! She said to herself. Bathing suit on, towel, yogurt, and book in hand, Miranda lay down on a lawn chair beside the pool and took a deep breath. She was going to enjoy at least an hour to herself and maybe read some of her book.

It was hard for outsiders to imagine how quiet and serene it could be in Loveladies on the lagoon, Miranda thought. In the mornings, especially, watching the sun come up over the houses and trees, the light reflecting images on the water as the tide came in; a lone squirrel scampering across the dock or seagulls flying overhead. The only sounds were the waves crashing on the beach or someone's wind chimes tinkling in the breeze. It was why one bought a house here. It was why one sat outside, hour after hour with a book and never got around to reading it. That was when the ennui would set in.

CHAPTER 7

Week of June 4

Liz had warned her that the construction noise would be bad, but she had not anticipated how relentless it would be. There appeared to be a number of different crews on the work site. Large tractor trailers were backing down Haverford's street, delivering the framing materials, or large dumpsters for all the construction debris. Mammoth dump trucks were unloading mounds of top soil needed to level the area on which the house would be built. There was grading equipment pushing earth, men raking or shoveling, shouting out instructions. All the while, they had music blaring so that they had something to listen to.

As the framing of the house began, other equipment was brought to the backyard. Apparently, they were having a pool dug too. All the activity just amazed Miranda. So many different projects going on at the same time!

Keslie Patch-Bohrod

CHAPTER 8

June 10 - Sunday

Haverford's building project started the week after their dinner at the Goldberg's. Hard to believe it was already June. Much to her dismay, the construction commotion was far noisier than she could have imagined. Sound carries on the lagoon. It really carries. Every hammer whack, saw whine, workers' swear word was heard by Miranda, even with the doors and windows closed. She had to turn up the TV in order to hear the programs. At least Jack and the kids were away working during the day. They would get home after the construction stopped. Miranda was there day in and day out, bombarded by noise, while she did laundry, cleaned and prepared meals. The only day it was supposed to be quiet was Sunday.

It really made her angry. She was supposed to be able to enjoy the quiet solitude of her home, but she couldn't. It was like they were doing everything in their power to make her leave, to drive her out or to drive her mad.

Jack had decided to take the boat out early that morning and the kids had to be in at work by seven thirty. There were some big catering jobs and they would be home late. Miranda decided to do some digging on the internet about Chicky Haverford.

First she found his obituary from the previous September. It had all the general information about where he was born, where he went to school and the family he left behind. What Miranda didn't know was that prior to his retirement, he worked in Washington, D.C. and Langley, Virginia in the C.I.A. and previously in the CIC (Counter Intelligence Corps). Of course, there were no details about what he did in either position.

The next thing she did was to call Liz and asked her to meet on the boulevard where they could go for a walk and talk. Miranda loved walking in the morning, especially when the sun was shining and there was a light breeze to keep her cool.

When they met at the end of Liz's street, the two women spent a few minutes complaining about the noise and dust. Being next door and with a row of trees as a sound barrier, Liz didn't hear as much as Miranda but had to deal with all the dirt flying everywhere. Her car was covered in a thick layer of dust, and her window screens were disgusting. Richard had warned her to keep a close eye on the hours of the workers and noise. He reminded her to check on the town website as to what was allowed and what wasn't. If they weren't complying with the town ordinances, she was to call the police or the town.

After wearing out that topic, Miranda switched gears and filled her in on the find from the obituary. She asked Liz if she knew any more about Chicky's background and previous employment. Liz was clueless but offered to ask Richard to do some digging. He had a few contacts that might provide some insight, although it might take a few days. He worked for an engineering consulting firm that had several government contracts. She really didn't understand what he did; it was a bit over her head and with some government business, it was confidential.

Miranda was hopeful for a quiet, restful day. But then the neighbors on the other side of the Haverford's property had a big Sunday cookout with music blaring, noisy kids and loud Jet Skis going up and down the lagoon. Jack just shook his head and offered to take Miranda to happy hour and dinner at Daymark in Barnegat Light.

Daymark was an upscale restaurant that was a favorite of theirs. It was always lively. They sat at the bar and had white wine and a wonderful octopus appetizer as they listened to Harper play her keyboard and sing. She was a talented young performer from the area and performed along the island at various restaurants during the dinner hour.

There were quite a few people at the bar; most were from their end of the island. They struck up conversations with two couples from Loveladies. After getting names, what street they lived on, lagoon or beachfront, how long they have been coming to this area for the summers, the conversation switched to something a bit disturbing. They had noticed things being a bit off within their homes. One of the wives said she was particular how items were arranged on their bookshelves, entertainment centers, and office. When they came down for Memorial Day weekend, she found things a bit askew. She did not have a housekeeper and had not had any work done on the house since last summer. The other couple complained of similar findings and also mentioned finding their personal computer had been plugged in. They swore they had left it unplugged when they were last down to protect it from any power surges that might happen if the electricity went out. Since they could find nothing missing, broken, or otherwise tampered with, they hadn't called the police.

Another neighbor had mentioned that in years past, the police had found people breaking into empty houses during the winter months and living there. It was hard to imagine someone would do that although, if you were homeless or were having money problems, it would be quite convenient. You just had to find a place that kept the heat and water on.

Another round of drinks came and the conversation shifted to the economy and who was employed where. The Cranford's both worked for Atlantic City Electric. Jim dealt with transmission and substations and Judy reported to the Senior Vice President of Government and External Affairs. Dave Walker worked for Amtrak in the IT department dealing with information security. Mary was a Pilate's instructor.

It was getting late, so Miranda and Jack said their goodbyes and returned home to find the kids sound asleep on the couch with TV on.

CHAPTER 9

Week of June 11 through15

Miranda had to call the town three times because the construction noise was going on beyond the allotted hours. She made sure Liz called too so it wouldn't seem like she was the only one being unreasonable.

The Craig's house was a modest one story structure nestled in between an old shoebox original home and a redone mega mansion. They had torn out the old kitchen a few years ago and they made sure to do it in the off season so the noise wouldn't bother anyone.

She had hated how the dining room table was attached to a short wall with the stove just to the right of it. Early on, this had been a big selling point for this style of house. The refrigerator was directly opposite the stove and every time you opened the refrigerator you banged your hip on that stupid wall. Miranda often commented that it was probably a man who designed the kitchen. Thankfully, they had been able to move the stove over to the other wall and put in a huge central island that would seat an army.

They had talked about doing more, but never got around to it. To them it just wasn't important; they didn't want to waste the time and it was all about enjoying the lagoon, family and friends. And who knew when another superstorm like Hurricane Sandy would come and wipe out the entire island and all the new renovations!

She wondered if the Haverford's were going to be like some of the families on Long Beach Island that had homes and only occasionally used them. There was one incredible home built on three lots by the ocean in Loveladies. Never once, had she seen anyone there. No one used the tennis court, or swam in the pool or sat in the gazebo that she ever saw. There were a slew of landscapers though. It was such a pity; to have a magnificent house and not use it. What good was money if you couldn't enjoy what it bought?

There were plenty of snow birds here. Those retired couples who arrived in April and then moved to their other warm weather home somewhere in the south around October. They seemed to make the best of their shore home.

Jack, being a wealth manager, already had plans to buy another home in the south for he and Miranda when they retired. They would keep the Loveladies property, but their primary residence would not have a New Jersey address. He would say "You can't retire in New Jersey with its tax requirements."

It was hard to be here in the winter anyway, only a few restaurants were open year round. Gas and groceries were hard to find on the island, resulting in long trips just to get food and fill the tank. And it was especially cold here in the winter, too. The wind, frozen lagoon, and few neighbors made for a dreary existence. The only thing you could do was watch TV and drink yourself into oblivion.

Miranda and Jack had come down a few times in past winters when they had kept the house open to get away. They had felt so isolated and shut in. They would see Alek and his wife Alina, who lived across the lagoon and to the right of them, and wondered how they managed it living here all year. She thought of the movie *The Shining* where the solitude led to cabin fever and the main character went basically crazy. How did Alek handle the aloneness, he surely couldn't go fishing everyday if it was snowing and sleeting?

CHAPTER 10

June 18 - Monday

Another week had gone by. Everyone had been busy with work and the time just seemed to slip away.

Miranda woke to find fog rolling in down the lagoon being pushed by ocean breezes. There was little visibility and it reminded her of yet another old movie of werewolves creeping about the moors. The forecast was for all day and all night rain, so thankfully, there would be little construction going on across the way.

The kids had been working hard all weekend and would probably sleep until past noon. They got Mondays off generally unless it was close to a holiday. Jack had gotten up at the crack of dawn to drive up North to start his work week. The house was clean and she couldn't take Maynard to the park or for a walk because it would be too wet and muddy. She certainly did not want to have to mop the floor again. The only quiet thing left to do was a jigsaw puzzle or read a book. She could read a book by herself, but she really wanted to talk with her neighbor.

Miranda called Liz to see if she was interested in helping her start a new puzzle she had picked up. She was anxious to hear if Richard had found out any more details about Chicky Haverford's death or his life in the CIA. Like Jack, Richard had left early to go to work leaving Liz to her own machinations.

By the time Liz arrived, Miranda had made a pot of coffee, put out some coffee cake and had dumped the new puzzle out of the box onto the table in the back room. She liked doing puzzles here because the room had six sliding glass doors that looked out on the neighbors and the lagoon. From this vantage point, she could keep an eye out on what was happening.

They worked quietly for a while, turning pieces right side up and collecting the border pieces. Liz stopped to enjoy her coffee and cake and watched Miranda as she sorted through the pieces, noting that she was also sorting by color and pattern.

"God, I didn't realize you were so OCD!" exclaimed Liz. "I thought we were just doing a stupid puzzle not cataloguing each piece according to size, shape, color, pattern and possible location coordinates! Are you going to set up stakes and string to form a grid like they do for archeological digs?"

Miranda laughed and said, "I don't have Obsessive Compulsive Disorder, but I guess you could say that I observe critical details. These two thousand piece puzzles can be quite daunting if you don't have a plan of attack. It saves a lot of time by sorting the pieces early. My goal is not to get frustrated but to be able to put the silly thing together! Just look at the picture on the box, we could be here all summer and not be able to finish it. The bottom half of the puzzle is all green grass with very little variation. That part will be a nightmare."

"Well, I still think you are nuts," muttered Liz. "Now, are you done concentrating on the puzzle and ready to hear what Richard found out about Chicky?"

Before Miranda could respond, they saw the Goldberg's neighbor, Alek Pronin go out in his boat. "Boy we have some strange ones on our lagoon. He goes out every day rain or shine and comes back at dinner. He either really loves fishing or he hates his wife," said Miranda. "I think they live here all year but I am not sure. When we come to the shore during the winter to check on the house, their house seems to be all shuttered up. Occasionally, we would see them. They don't have too many friends, although I have seen them spending time with Frederick next door."

"Now, there is another strange one. I see that guy out in his yard of river rock raking his stones. Is he into Zen gardening?" wondered Liz. "I don't get it. He can hardly walk, he is about ninety, that is dead in dog years, and he rakes his rocks."

Laughing, Miranda said, "Jack's parents, when they owned this house, knew Frederick. Apparently, he is a Jewish psychiatrist from Philadelphia. He was educated in South America and came to work in the United States quite a few years ago. I really don't know much about him, he exchanges pleasantries with me but pretty much keeps to himself. Maybe the raking of the rocks is a combination of weeding and exercise, because jogging and water sports are out of his league? I always joke with Jack that Frederick is really a Nazi in hiding, coming from South America and all. You know that's where they fled after World War II. He gets so mad at me and says 'For God's sake, he's Jewish!' and I say, 'What better cover!'

Liz is beside herself with laughter. "I can't believe you! You see intrigue in every corner."

"Oh, you think I joke about possible intrigue, but did you know that Loveladies was built by Russian spies?" asks Miranda.

"You have got to be kidding!" exclaims Liz. But when she sees the serious look on Miranda's face she says, "I really know very little about the island and how things started here."

"I remember reading that in an article years ago that Jack showed me about Loveladies," says Miranda. "How about we go to the library instead of starting this puzzle and we will see if we can track it down. I really don't know that much either. They have to have books about Long Beach Island. We can ask the Reference Librarian to help us look. On the way there, you can tell me what Richard found out about Chicky."

Keslie Patch-Bohrod

CHAPTER 11

June 18 - Monday

The library was about ten minutes away which was more than enough time for Liz to tell Miranda that Chicky's past work with the CIA was inaccessible by Richard. She reported, "He did confirm that he worked and lived in Virginia, had just retired from his job, and moved permanently here to the island. Richard was surprised to find his vocational history was so hush-hush. Maybe he was part of some covert operations on behalf of the government? He also mentioned that there was a lot of funny business going on during the time Chicky would have been employed. The Cold War was in full bloom, World War II was over, Nazis were being chased all over the world, and the nation was scared to death of the Soviets.

Miranda said, "Now look who is full of intrigue! But all those things would be interesting to research."

They parked the car in the parking lot and entered the small island library. Not sure how much information they would be able to find, they went in search of a Reference Librarian who might help them track down the article and maybe some books about Long Beach Island.

They discovered Diane, the Reference Librarian, was quite eager to help. She informed them, "I don't get many requests here because it is such a small library. As you can imagine it can get pretty boring. We have summer reading programs for kids and adults but that only takes up a few hours every day. The information you are looking for sounds quite exciting and will be something some of my adult readers might be interested in too. While I am searching through my archives online, why don't the two of you start with our section of books on Long Beach Island history?" She pointed the two in the right direction, and then fired up her computer to start her own search.

Miranda and Liz found a number of books that provided them with the basics of the island and Loveladies in specific. Miranda told Liz "What I personally know is that people on our lagoon come from various locations and from different ethnic backgrounds. That is what Loveladies is all about. It had originally been a haven for Communists, gays, Jews and artists. Currently, we have people from Pennsylvania, New Jersey, Delaware, New York, Virginia and even Germany. The ethnicity includes Jewish, Italian, Argentinian, German and one person has direct ties to the Mayflower!"

They each started reading and taking notes agreeing that they would talk about what they found tomorrow morning over coffee and the puzzle. Diane came in search of the two about thirty minutes later and handed Miranda the article she remembered reading years ago. Miranda shouted, "I can't believe you found it!" Then she realized she was in a library and immediately apologized to the readers around her.

Diane informed her that she really had to search, finally finding it in the old archives for the magazine where it had originally been printed. "I just skimmed through it, but it looks like a doozy of an article. I can't wait to read the one I printed out for myself. Please let me know if there is anything else I can help with."

Miranda and Liz thanked her profusely and finished up their own research. Liz, completing her last set of notes with a flourish states, "Miranda, I have to get back home. I have to run some errands and get to Costco before the hordes descend. Is there anything you need while I am there?" Miranda replied no and that she would be going out that way on Wednesday.

Today, she too had to get home. She had promised Erica to take her shopping at the South end of the island in Beach Haven while Kevin watched Totenham versus Chelsea soccer on TV. Kevin had been a top ranking soccer player in high school but decided his education and sleep was much more important than playing on his college soccer team. He also was afraid of serious sports injuries and at twenty-two, didn't like the idea of knee surgeries or concussions. He would just have to enjoy the sport vicariously on the couch.

CHAPTER 12

June 18 - Monday

Later that day as they started driving to the other end of the island, Erica asked what her mother and their neighbor had been doing all morning. Miranda filled her in on their search for knowledge of all things Loveladies.

Erica rolled her eyes and said, "You guys are so weird. Nothing ever goes on in Loveladies. It is the most boring spot on the island. There are no restaurants, bars, shops, or businesses of any kind. I can't see why anyone would want to own a house here. Thank god the township started the LBI shuttle, that way kids can get around the island and do things if they can't drive or don't want to drive because they are going to be drinking alcohol."

"That's the point, Erica," Miranda explained, "some people want quiet. They want a haven where they can get away from their troubles and relax. I know it was hard when you kids were young. There weren't too many kids in the area. So we had to go the beach or invite some of your friends down. You and Kevin were always begging us to take you to Fantasy Island in Beach Haven so you could ride the rides, play in the arcade, or play mini golf. We would have taken you more often but it would take us forty-five minutes to get there with all the traffic and low speed limits."

"Mom, my best memories are when the cousins would come. We would have so much fun riding our tricycles and bikes up and down our street. Someone would yell, 'Car!' and we would immediately go over to the side and wait for them to go by. We would run out to greet the ice cream truck and each get a Power Ranger ice cream bar that turned the skin around our mouth bright red or blue. Then Dad and Uncle Doug would take us into the outdoor shower, shouting 'One done daughter or one done son!" when they were done scrubbing us down, then ushering us out to the waiting assembly line of towels of Grandma, you or Aunts Mary and Ruth."

Miranda reminded Erica, "We have had some excitement over the years here, in case you forgot. Remember last summer when I yelled to everyone to grab a lawn chair and beer and meet me by the dock? Alek was putting up a tall ladder against one of his dying pine trees. His wife was steadying the ladder as he climbed up, holding the ladder in one hand and big chain saw in the other. I told everyone to hurry up the show was about to begin. We readied our chairs and side tables with our beer and Alek climbed higher and higher."

"You know that scene brings back a memory of one of my favorite movies, *The Burbs,* Tom Hanks, Carrie Fisher, Bruce Dern, Corey Feldman, and Henry Gibson. I don't remember the characters' names so bear with me. Tom Hanks is on vacation and he and his neighbors suspect something sinister is going on in one of the houses on the cul-de-sac. A young kid played by Corey Feldman, who lived on the block would invite friends over to hang on his porch and watch the chaos and mayhem in his neighborhood. In the end, they find the neighbor had really been killing people. So us sitting there watching Alek was like that kid with his friends on his porch watching the crazy activities on the lagoon."

"Anyway, much to our dismay, Alek failed to cut off any of his own limbs while trimming the limbs of his tree. But it was another enjoyable afternoon with my family. There is nothing better in my book then being nosy and watching the neighbors!"

"Yes, I remember that. It was one of the only times we saw him during the day. He's always out on his boat fishing," recalled Erica.

"Oh, and remember when the Stein's boat was leaking oil and they got all bent out of shape because someone called the EPA on them? Or when Dad woke us in the middle of the night telling us to come into the room by the pool? When we get in there, we see the Stein's brand new custom BBQ center up in flames. We watched as all the neighbors came out, the fire departments from Barnegat Light and Harvey Cedars came to put out the flames. Not the Goldman's but the neighbors on the other side of Stein's were so worried that the fire would spread to their trees and eventually to their house. The wind was blowing in that direction and it was a real possibility. They never found out how it happened. We always thought it was one of the kids had left food on the grill and hadn't turned it off. But that did not make sense. How would that cause such a big fire?

Maybe that and the oil leak were connected. They are the most annoying people on the lagoon. Maybe someone was trying to send them a message. They have no clue how noisy they are. One thing was for certain, everyone was out watching except Alek or his wife. I don't understand why they wouldn't come out to see what was going on, especially with the sirens from the fire trucks. Whenever there is a fire, everyone is worried it might spread to their property." Erica just shrugged her shoulders indicating she didn't know either.

Miranda and Erica spent the rest of the day shopping and returned home to start dinner. The kids both worked the next day so Miranda and Liz could review the information they found out about Long Beach Island and Loveladies. After the dishes were all done and the kitchen was cleaned up, Miranda settled in to read the article Diane printed for her about how two suspected Russian spies had been the property developers for Loveladies.

Keslie Patch-Bohrod

CHAPTER 13

June 19 - Tuesday

Liz showed up bright and early with her notes in hand and as she came in through the door Miranda greeted and handed her a cup of coffee and suggested she sit at the kitchen island. She had all of her notes and the articles spread out on the table. Liz started them off with what she had found out.

"This is so fun, it reminds me of when I was in grade school and had to stand in front of the class and do show and tell or give a book report on Abraham Lincoln!"

"Loveladies is a small area on Long Beach Island that is part of Long Beach Township and we are located between Harvey Cedars and Barnegat Light. We have no businesses to speak of here but we do have a private tennis club and the Long Beach Island Foundation of the Arts and Sciences which started about 1948. This was why all the artsy fartsy people wanted to live here. Over the years, they have really developed into a great place to explore your artistic talents, enjoy music performances and even take some classes. "

"The Island is about eighteen miles long, with Harvey Cedars being one fifth of a mile across and the widest part of the island is only half a mile wherever that is. Hunters came here in the 1690s. The first lighthouse was built in 1835 in Barnegat Light because of the dangerous inlet and the current lighthouse, "Old Barney" was built later. Speaking of Old Barney, have you ever climbed up to the top? We counted the stairs one time, two hundred seventeen steps! There is a great view of the inlet and people love to fish off the jetty. There were some United States Life Saving Stations built in these parts, one in Barnegat Light in the early 1870s which is about where the United States Coast Guard Station is now located. There was another one built in 1875. There was a small island in the bay by the station that was owned by Thomas Lovelady. Over the years the name morphed into Loveladies."

"There have been a number of bad storms over the years in 1920, 1923, 1935, and the 1962 Ash Wednesday storm which almost wiped out the island," Liz continued. "Then of course, we know Hurricane Sandy in October of 2012, where there was over one billion dollars in damage. We were very fortunate living here because our beaches in Loveladies had been replenished and the dunes were in good shape which supposedly protected all the properties here quite well. Not like in Harvey Cedars where some ocean front homeowners refused to allow dune replenishment because it required public access to their beaches. Because of their selfishness, the resulting damage to other homes was massive."

"Oh, and I also found that there were five people attacked by sharks, of which four were killed along the Jersey Shore in 1916. The first one was off Beach Haven.

Miranda asked, "Did you find any reference to Mary Lee, the Great White shark that visits our waters? The kids say there is a tracker app you can download to your phone to see where she is swimming. I also know there is a website that lets you track in real time the location of a bunch of sharks. Mary Lee is sixteen feet long and I think she was near the Jersey shore recently. I had also heard that one of those shark attacks you just mentioned had taken place in Matawan Creek which is weird. They thought that because there was a full moon that the salinity of the water increased thus allowing the shark to survive swimming in that area. If that is true, maybe sharks could make it to the lagoons? Do you want to go for a dip later? "

Liz shuddered and said, "I'll pass. I haven't been in the ocean since watching the movie *Jaws* in the mid-1970s."

Miranda cleared her throat and began, "Now to the really good information! According to what Diane printed out for us, Nathan Gregory Silvermaster and William Ludwig (Lud) Ullmann were suspected Communist spies working within the United States Government.

"Just to summarize some of the information," Miranda began, "Silvermaster was born 1898 and died in 1964. He was Jewish from Odessa, Russia and came to the United States in 1914. He attended two Universities in the U.S. studying Economics. He was an active member of the Community Party; married a woman named Elena

(Helen) Witte in 1930, and was believed to have been recruited by Jacob Golos as a soviet agent. In 1935, he worked for the Federal Resettlement Administration which was part of the Agricultural Department. The couple became friendly with William 'Lud' Ullmann, also employed within the U.S. Government. The three of them bought a house together and it was rumored Ullmann was having an affair with Silvermaster's wife or maybe it was a ménage a trois. Later when Ullmann was working in the Treasury Department, he was suspected of spying for the Soviets."

"During World War II it was alleged that Silvermaster turned over important details to the Soviets with regards to U.S. and German military forces and plans. In 1942, he was suspected of being a spy by the House Un-American Activities Committee but nothing could be confirmed. An economic advisor close to President Roosevelt, Lauchlin Currie was able to put a stop to the investigation. I guess he had a friend in high places. Silvermaster then got a job with the War Production Board which gave him information on arms production, which he allegedly passed to the Soviets. In 1945 a woman named Elizabeth Bentley, a fellow spy who had come to their house on numerous occasions to pick up documents and microfilm, was questioned by the FBI. She turned over names of Soviet spies, with Silvermaster and Ullmann high on the list. During the early 1940s she would go to their house in Washington D.C. and obtain rolls of film that she brought back to New York City in her knitting bag to her boyfriend, Jacob Golos, the same person who supposedly got Silvermaster involved in spying."

"A knitting bag?" laughed Liz.

"What's so funny about that? "Questioned Miranda, sounding offended. "When I was an insurance investigator, I got my best video by hiding my video camera in a diaper bag. Remember how big those suckers used to be the 1980s? I would put it down next me, say on a park bench, and get all sorts of incriminating evidence of the so called seriously injured mom's and dad's as they were out running around with their kids at some park. No one was the wiser. I would just sit there pretending my baby was asleep in the carriage, even though this was before we had kids. Just like me, this Elizabeth Bentley was sitting on the train or however she got back to the city, carrying secret documents and microfilm in a knitting bag, looking all normal. I'm sure not many people even paid attention to her."

"Because she named them to the FBI, in 1948, they were called before the House Un-American Activities Committee but would not answer any questions, pleading the fifth. They were never prosecuted, apparently, they had someone high enough on the food chain that vouched for and protected them."

Liz just sat there with her mouth open. "I just can't believe that! I see that Diane wrote down the names of other books and articles written about them and other Soviet spies of the time. It is just unimaginable that nothing was done to them. Wasn't this during the McCarthy era? So what happened that they ended up in Loveladies?"

"As I understand it," began Miranda, "it was hard for them to get work being that they were suspected spies. So they had to find something on their own. The three of them, still together, lived in a house in Harvey Cedars beginning in 1947. They bought two hundred fifty acres in Loveladies, dredged out lagoons, and started building houses on hundred by hundred feet of lagoon space, which makes it great for people like us who want to have a boat."

"People from Philadelphia began to buy their houses, many of them artists of some sort. Then psychologist and psychiatrists began to buy here. I remember talking with some of the older residents here in Loveladies and they referred to Loveladies as having the nickname 'Couch Cove', back then because of all the psychologists and psychiatrists. I wonder if that is when Frederick bought his house. Remember, I told you he was a psychiatrist? Ullmann continued to be suspected of spying and was called to testify during the late 1940s and 1950s. After the big storm in 1962, Ullmann built his own home on Pompano Drive and the Silvermasters moved near the Long Beach Island Foundation of the Arts and Sciences. Maybe by that time, they had had enough of each other!"

Liz thought for a moment then said, "If they kept calling Ullmann to testify, maybe that means they kept suspecting him (or them) of continuing to spy. They wouldn't just stop cold turkey would they? Russia most certainly still wanted and needed the information they had been supplying. They hadn't been caught and arrested. They were just questioned; it was Elizabeth Bentley's word against theirs. They would still need agents to gather information and forward it. Would Silvermaster and Ullmann be fired right off or would they wait to see what happened to them. You would have to imagine they would be watched constantly even though they could no longer work in the United States government. They were probably hounded out of D.C."

"If that would have happened today, the journalists would be all over them especially CNN and Fox news, at least until a bigger, better story came along. Back then, maybe it was written up in the D.C. papers and a regional paper. Was it national news?"

"The Cold War was all about secrets and subterfuge. They were good at hiding what they were doing. As long as they weren't put in jail, they could have continued but with more care and ingenuity. Maybe that's why they developed the Loveladies connection. There were plenty of left wing sympathizer types going to Long Beach Island. So maybe they recruited other communists, possibly people who were buying their houses in Loveladies and the Silvermaster spy ring continued? The types of people that were buying down here at the time were part of that wild, free thinking and living age of beatniks."

"When did Frederick buy his house?" asked Liz. "He is a psychiatrist originally from another country right? Could he be a Communist? I know you thought he was a Nazi. There are quite a few people on our lagoon alone that might be the right age. So let's think about the math. If someone was in their twenties in the 1960s they would be in their late seventies or early eighties. If they were in their thirties, they would be in their nineties. Frederick is that old. Would he have had enough money in his late twenties to early thirties to buy a house in Loveladies at that time? Alek would have been in his twenties… and that's just our lagoon! I wonder how many original owners are still here."

"Wow, that's a lot to think about. OK," considered Miranda, "so let's say Silvermaster and Ullmann somehow recruited young spies that either lived down here or they set them up in houses in Loveladies. They had lost their network that had been in place, since Elizabeth Bentley was no longer transporting their documents or microfilm. A new network and means for transferring the information had to be developed. Elizabeth Bentley used to hide the microfilm in her knitting bag. Maybe the creation of the lagoons had something to do with a possible new plan. I find it strange that economists all of a sudden take up dredging and building quaint little houses don't you? I don't think those skills are part of your standard economics curriculum."

"Our lagoons empty into Barnegat Bay which leads right to the Atlantic Ocean. Maybe they transported information by boat?" Miranda continued, "Remember this was the beginning of the Cold War. Everyone was spying on each other; no one was trusted. I don't remember much from history class, but I do remember bomb shelters and the drills in elementary school. We were terrified. Then things calmed down but there was always the Communist threat. So I imagine, over the years, the spying and passing of information never stopped."

Miranda then told Liz about something she read not too long ago about the FBI warning that Russians may have somehow installed malware on computers. It was suggested that everyone unplug their routers, then reconnect, and somehow the FBI could trace the IP address of the hackers. "I have also read that the Russians still have operational spies in the United States going after economic information. You know about the investigation into the recent presidential election. They could try to disrupt Wall Street, the banking system or even take down our power grids. Who knows? Maybe the Silvermaster/Ullmann spy ring, could still be collecting economic data since that had been their original vocation?"

"With all this talk of espionage, it makes me wonder about Chicky's death," said Liz. "He worked for the CIA for years, so maybe there is some kind of crazy connection here."

Miranda thought for a minute then said, "Maybe he was placed here, to keep tabs on things; keep an eye open. The CIA and FBI had to be aware that Silvermaster and Ullmann settled here and started a business. They had to keep watching just in case. What was going on here all these years? Why didn't they ever find anything?"

"Getting back to Chicky's death, if it wasn't an accident or suicide, then who could have killed him? The most logical would be someone who lived on this lagoon or close by so he or she could see when Chicky went into the water and of course would need to be a good swimmer.

Or they knew he would be going for his swim in the morning and cut through someone's property or swam into our lagoon prior to Chicky getting into the water. That person could have come from anywhere. There is always someone swimming up and down the lagoon, some even swim into the other channels. So let's think about this. Who do we know that swims in the lagoon on a regular basis? Chicky was the only one from the Haverford family. I see Alek's wife ease into the water after she is working in her garden. She usually just floats around on her noodle for a while then gets out. I don't see her as a particularly strong swimmer. Every once in a while I will see Alek out there swimming and he is very fit for a man his age. There are two men who live down on the end of your street that swim, but they don't spend much time down here. Frederick is never in the water. You won't catch me dead swimming in that lagoon! Sorry, bad choice of words."

Liz giggled and said, "Same here!"

"If we would have been here last Labor Day Weekend, I would have seen someone. Maynard always barks at the swimmers and kayakers which alerts me. Frankly, he barks at anything around the back yard and lagoon. I have to run out and quiet him down so he doesn't disturb the neighbors too much. I also worry that he might jump in and go after whoever is swimming. "

"You know how dangerous he is with his long talons! Remember when Kevin had to jump into the lagoon after Maynard? They had been boating at Tice's Shoal with him and he was still so excited about going on the boat and swimming with everyone there. Maynard spotted the neighbors next door in the lagoon with their noodles and must have thought they were back at Tice's and jumped right off the boat. I had to yell to the neighbors to try to push him away so they wouldn't get scratched. Kevin was able to swim to him and hold onto his doggie life vest. By the time Kevin manhandled him up on the Jet Ski ramp, he was covered in deep scratches. Hey, that reminds me, our neighbors next door go in the lagoon all the time and they are from Virginia- the CIA is in Langley, Virginia. But didn't you say they weren't here Labor Day? Maybe whoever it was, had to wait until we left, giving them opportunity without being observed."

Miranda gave Liz a worried look, "We should be careful who we speak to about Chicky's death, especially if we voice our opinion that he was murdered. We may not be safe if whoever is responsible for his death thinks we are digging and getting close to his or her identity.

CHAPTER 14

June 20, 21, and 22 - Wednesday through Friday

Miranda spent the rest of the week working on the outside of the house. With company coming the beginning of July for their big summer party, she wanted the yard and flower beds to look nice.

Over Memorial Day weekend, she and Jack had taken care of the front planting areas. Since this was what everyone saw, they always tried to tackle that first. It was really a pain in the neck to trim down the bushes and trees. The town required that limbs be cut no longer than 4 feet, and then bound with twine or string, making it easier for the waste management workers to collect them. Maybe next week she would try to plant some pretty annuals.

The tomatoes, cucumbers and herbs had also been put in and were doing nicely, as were the weeds. They seemed to be everywhere. She pulled the biggest ones and sprayed the smaller ones with a solution of Dawn detergent, salt and white vinegar. She refused to use Roundup, because when it rained there was runoff from their land into the lagoon and because Maynard had a tendency to eat crabgrass. He got enough pesticides with his flea medication he didn't need to eat it too.

Friday, she decided Maynard needed a treat. She felt guilty neglecting him with all the yard work she had been doing. Barnegat Light had a great, fenced-in dog park that he loved.

As soon as she got him into the car, he knew something was up. When she turned left onto the boulevard, he knew where they were going and began to cry, whine and bark. It just amazed her how perceptive he was.

Once inside the park, Miranda sat on one of the benches while Maynard did his thing. He enjoyed sniffing the other dogs, checking out the nooks and crannies of the dugouts (the park used to be a softball field) and generally meandering around the fence line. A local artist had put up huge paintings he had done of different dog breeds along the back fence. It was a nice place to hang out. Other dog owners were very friendly and there were always a number of conversations going on around the park.

The park was near Viking Village, where the fishing fleet brought in the catch of the day and by the Coast Guard Station. She saw and heard one of the orange helicopters flying overhead approaching the waterway. It hovered for a few minutes, and then lowered what looked like a man in a harness into the water near a jet ski. One dog owner told her that they were practicing their search and rescue maneuvers.

She imagined with all the water sports in this area, boating, swimming, kayaking, and jet skiing the Coast Guard got a big workout. And, being on the Atlantic Ocean, they must also see their share of immigration enforcement, drug smuggling and a slew of other crimes. Their bright orange helicopters could be seen on a regular basis flying up and down the coast line and assisting in all sorts of water rescues and missions.

Nearby, she also recalled, was Fort Dix, McGuire Air Force Base and the Naval Air Engineering Station. Kevin had played in many soccer tournaments at the base. Being on a military base, getting in and out had been such a pain in the ass, especially after 9/11. A week didn't go by without seeing fighter jets, huge cargo planes and military helicopters flying overhead, either heading due east out to the Atlantic or due West back to the base. Knowing the base was so close both reassured and scared her to death. It was there for protection but it was also a target, she realized.

CHAPTER 15

June 25 - Monday

June seemed to come and go so quickly and the July fourth holiday was approaching. The Craigs would host their annual party for the neighborhood, bring in catered food, some local musician, and when it got dark enough, they would climb to their roof top deck and watch the fireworks from the surrounding towns. It was always lots of fun and each year, more and more people attended. Miranda had already emailed the neighbors before Memorial Day to hold the date. The kids turned in the catering order on their first day back at work and Jack had contacted a woman that would play her steel drums for the party. There was nothing left to do until a few days before the gathering.

It was the last Monday of the month and it had been uncharacteristically quiet. Miranda was deep into one of her books. She thoroughly enjoyed mysteries and thrillers. Occasionally, she would read a Cozy Mystery, especially the ones that included recipes as part of the story. This one in particular had a sandwich combination and she decided she would make it later. She didn't often eat deli meats but this sounded really good: salami, arugula, sliced red onion with mayonnaise on a multi-grained roll. Maybe she would also include a very cold bottle of Heineken. That would be dinner! As she continued to read in glorious silence, her quiet was interrupted when she saw and heard large backhoe front loader type vehicles coming onto Chicky's backyard. They were carrying large, long pilings and were laying them along the edge of the property close to the lagoon. Miranda knew immediately what was transpiring. The workers would be installing a new bulkhead and dock. This would not be a small or quiet undertaking.

Miranda started closing the sliding glass doors in the room that overlooked the pool and lagoon, as more and more dust was churned in the air by the moving heavy equipment. She closed her book and moved over to the table where she and Liz had been working on the jigsaw puzzle. She absent mindedly began working on the puzzle as

75

the men continued their work. She was amazed at the process of putting in the pilings for the bulkhead. Moments later a barge that just fit in the lagoon was positioned by the deft hands of the operator at the back of the Haverford's property.

Liz had gone back home with Richard on Sunday. Richard would go to work that week while Liz did chores around their primary home, grocery shop and purchase a gift for a wedding they were attending that next Saturday. She would drive their second car back to the shore the following Monday. In the meantime, she was missing all the festivities.

Jack had gotten up at five that morning and drove north to his office, where he would shower and shave, eat breakfast then start his Monday back at work. The kids had reluctantly gotten up at seven, dressed in their shorts and Antonio's T-shirts, and stumbled into the kitchen. Since they were both working the same shift today, they decided to take one car. They would stop and pick up a coffee and bagel along the way for their breakfast. Maynard was there, of course, but he would seclude himself on the one of the kids' beds and sleep most of the day, oblivious to the world around him.

Miranda was alone but felt as if the world was coming down around her as the machines began to drive the pilings into the lagoon bed. It was as if she were along the San Andreas Fault line. Everything was shaking. She could hear the wine glasses in the china cabinet clink against one another. The house vibrated even though the activity was taking place across the lagoon. She began to wonder if their foundation and gunite pool had the potential to crack with the ground quaking as it was. The pounding and noise was relentless. She watched for over two hours and they were nowhere near done. She could not take it anymore; she had to get out of there. Her best option was go to go to the library where it was bound to be quiet. It would also give her a chance to chat with Diane and possibly get some help in researching a few ideas that she had been thinking about.

CHAPTER 16

June 25 - Monday

When Miranda arrived at the library around eleven thirty, a swarm of kids and mothers were leaving after attending one of the summer reading programs. They would grab lunch before heading off to the beach or some other summer time activity. She was grateful the main room was essentially empty of people. This would give her the opportunity to pick Diane's brain.

As she approached the main desk, Diane was unwrapping her sandwich. Miranda said, "Hi Diane, I'm sorry to interrupt your lunch, but I wonder if you would help me find books or articles on a few subjects."

Diane, with sandwich up to her mouth said, "I would love to, but could you please give me ten minutes at least to eat? I have been really busy this morning with our summer program and I am starving! If I don't eat, I might take a bite out of your arm."

Miranda laughed and said, "Of course, I'm sorry that I interrupted. Can I use the computers over there to start some internet searches?"

"Of course, the login information is on the laminated card next to the keyboard. I will be with you just as soon as I wolf down this sandwich and go the bathroom."

Miranda had brought a pad of paper with her and began writing down criteria she would enter into her Google search. She would share this with Diane. She began to create a numbered list based on everything she and Liz had been talking about.

1. CIA and CIC: Where Chicky had worked.
2. Nazis and South America: Suspicions about Frederick and his background
3. Russian spies- current spies and any other information about Russia and its present activities in America. (Assuming Silvermaster/Ullmann spy ring was real and still existed.)
4. Nazis still sought and those recently captured: Again, suspicions about Frederick.

Miranda was from Ohio originally and remembered being shocked to learn the story of John Demjanjuk, thought to be Ivan the Terrible, responsible for killing over twenty-eight thousand Jews at Sobibor. He had lived in Cleveland. There had been deportations, trials, multiple charges, overturned verdicts, conviction, but he died in 2012 before he could be sentenced. He had been hiding in plain sight. She added that to her search criteria.

Her comments to Jack about Frederick came back to her. Maybe she could find information about Nazis hiding as Jews. She tried to remember the details of a TV mystery where a Nazi, had been hiding as a Jew. When the war was ending and the Allied troops were nearing the camp where he was a guard. He persuaded another guard to tattoo his arm. He then changed into a striped prisoner uniform and was later led out with the surviving Jewish prisoners. She wasn't sure this was the exact story but in reality something like that could have happened.

Miranda felt overwhelmed by the amount of questions she had and her lack of knowledge. Were any of her concerns really possible? Could there still be Russian spies or escaped Nazi war criminals on LBI? Was she being silly and naïve, she was sure Jack would think so. Would Liz be interested in pursuing these topics with her or would she get bored and beg to be left alone? Or would this just be a crazy exercise in Cold War history.

There wasn't anything pressing she had to do other than the housekeeping chores which were never ending. And with all the noise from the construction, she really needed something to distract her and keep her busier than normal. That was the problem with living in Loveladies. If you didn't work, she didn't count the endless and mindless jobs of the homemaker, then there really wasn't much to keep your mind occupied. One just went about one's activities in a zombie state, or drank heavily.

She finally decided. What would it hurt to research this stuff? It would be educational to say the least and maybe, just maybe, she would find out something. She could even have conversations with Jack about World War II and maybe she would enjoy watching the History Channel with him, two of his passions.

Diane saw Miranda staring off into the distance. She had seen this expression many times before. "Miranda, can I help you get started on your search? I see you have a list. May I have a look at it?"

Miranda handed the list to Diane. She whistled and said, "Boy, these are some topics! Are you researching a book or working on a thesis?"

Miranda, not wanting to divulge what she was really doing, just replied, "No, the article you printed out for me just seemed to raise more questions than answers. I am not having much luck finding the type of information or answers I am looking for."

"Just give me a few minutes and I will work through your list. I will just print out whatever I can quickly find to get you started then do more research if you need me to. I also think we have a book about Nazis escaping after the war that you might be interested in. I will go pull that from the shelf and you can begin to look it over while I do the rest."

A few minutes later Diane returned with a book and suggested Miranda find a comfortable chair and begin to read it while she continued her research.

She had only gotten through about twenty pages of the introduction when Diane handed her a stack of articles and a bill for the printing costs. Miranda pulled out her wallet and handed Diane a ten dollar bill. After receiving her change, she thanked Diane for all her help and headed home to begin her research.

CHAPTER 17

June 25 - Monday

Being a Monday, there weren't too many people on the island. Miranda stopped off at Antonio's and picked up some salami and bread for her dinner. The kids had gone in to work just in case things picked up but told her they had the next day off because it was so slow and planned to go visit friends overnight. They would come home after work, pick up their clothes and leave, returning Tuesday at dinner time.

Miranda made it back home quickly, let Maynard out to do his business and decided to have her sandwich for lunch. She knew Jack had some bottles of Heineken in another refrigerator they kept in the outdoor shed.

She sliced the large red onion and smeared mayonnaise on the multi-grained roll. She layered the salami and onion evenly on the bread. She checked on Maynard, who was lying in the sun on the deck, as she retrieved the ice cold Heineken from the fridge. She took her lunch into the back room and sat at the table. The construction crew was still working on the bulkhead but the pounding had stopped. Electrical saws, however, were in constant use.

As she ate, she began to look through the stack of reading material Diane had provided. As the noise continued outside, she realized there would be no way she could concentrate.

Watching the workers move from the barge to the dock and then into the house, Miranda had an idea. What if she could prove how easy it was to get in someone's house or to kill Chicky? Maybe she could do it by slipping into the lagoon at night or even during the day without being noticed? With the Goldbergs gone this week and the kids not coming home, it would be the perfect time to test her idea. She would sneak into their home and leave them a note. They would never press charges against her if she got caught. It would serve as a wakeup call that their key should never be hidden on their property.

She suspected Liz would leave a key in the outdoor shower or under a pot of flowers or something, even after Miranda's story of the break-in. They were always having work done on their house while they were away.

Miranda and Jack learned long ago not to do this. Their shore house had been broken into by using the key they hid in the shower. They suspected it was one of the construction workers in the neighborhood at the time but couldn't prove it. After that happened, if a contractor or someone had to enter their home to do work during the off season, Miranda would mail the key to them with a self-addressed, stamped envelope. The work would be done and the key would be mailed back to them. She would keep a record of who received the key, when it was returned and if something happened, this information could be given to the police to investigate. At any time during the summer, she or Jack would always be here and monitor whoever was doing the work.

Having never done anything like this before, Miranda had to put on her breaking and entering cap. Did she walk over, going around the block or did she swim over. She certainly didn't want to drive over and leave the car parked near the house. If she walked, there was a greater chance that someone would see her or her image might be picked up on an outside home security camera. The Goldbergs didn't have outdoor cameras and she assumed if the neighbors did, they wouldn't pick her up because she wasn't on their property. Kayaking or rowing would make too much noise, plus their kayak was bright yellow and easily seen even in the dark. She would have to swim. If she swam over, she would drip water everywhere. Maybe she could put a towel in a big Ziploc bag so it wouldn't get wet. She would climb out of the water and dry off before entering the Goldberg's home. Yes, that's what she would try.

Sunset was around eight thirty that night. She would have to wait until it was really dark, say ten. Thankfully, there would not be a full moon, reducing the chance that someone would see her as well as sharks swimming in the lagoons.

CHAPTER 18

June 25 - Monday night

At nine forty-five, Miranda put on her bathing suit and found a towel that would fit in the extra-large Ziploc bag. She folded it into a small square and shoved it in, squeezing the top sections together to form an airtight closure. All the house lights needed to be turned off so no one would see her exiting the house. Maynard was dead asleep, having eaten an entire rawhide bone after his dinner and was on the couch on the other side of the house.

The bedroom sliding glass door was the quietest to open and close, so that was her exit point. She crouched down and moved over the back yard, careful to walk on the pavers, not the loose stones which made a crunching noise when walked upon. As she approached the end of the dock, she looked around at the houses that lined the lagoon in both directions. Only a few had their inside lights on, no one was outside that she could tell and it was very quiet and thankfully dark.

She couldn't believe she was actually going to do this. Never in the many years of living in this house had she been in the lagoon. The kids and their friends would go in all time, and would try to coax her into joining them. There was something about dark, murky water that gave her the willies. The bottom was not visible and there were fish- lots of fish, slimy fish. She shuddered at the thought of fish rubbing up against her skin. Even more frightening would be jellyfish stinging her. One year, the kids had even caught an eel in the crab trap. She thought back to the conversation she had with Liz about the shark found in the Matawan Creek and hoped the salinity in the lagoon was really low.

Pushing aside her fear and repulsion, she eased into the water very slowly. Miranda began to breast stroke across the lagoon. It wasn't very far but the water was still cold this time of year. She climbed up the Goldberg's ladder, careful of the barnacles on the steps of the ladder that could shred her feet. The outdoor shower was on the right side of the house and she was thankful the key was exactly where she thought it would be. She unzipped the bag and took out the towel. The cool night air, wet skin, and nerves made her shiver violently. The towel did the job of removing the water from her body, but the bathing suit and her hair were still wet. Her teeth were chattering so much she was convinced the whole lagoon could hear her.

What she hadn't considered, was that the key went to the front door. The front door was bathed in light from the fixture directly above it. Shit. She could be seen entering the house if someone across the street looked out their window. The light would need to be put out. Liz was going to kill her. She had to break the light.

Picking up stones from the side yard, Miranda started throwing them at the light. After nine attempts, she finally succeeded in breaking the light leaving the front porch in darkness and littered with a bunch of glass and rocks.

Waiting a few minutes to make sure none of the neighbors had heard the glass breaking, she moved carefully to the door avoiding the glass shards, inserted the key, and entered the house. She made sure to relock the front door. The Goldbergs had a home office on the main floor where Richard did work when he was at the shore. She made her way to the back room, fumbling around by the minimal light from the street light through the window. Richard had a stack of Post-It notes next to his computer. Miranda took one and wrote, *Hi Richard, just wanted you to know that I broke into your house using your hidden shower key and now I know all of your secrets hidden on your computer. I did not find, however, the porn sites you frequent!*

Miranda decided not to risk going out the front door. She found a back door she could lock as she exited. Slipping into the lagoon, she let out a sigh of relief that she had accomplished getting into the Goldberg's home without getting spotted or arrested. Dripping wet, she crouched and duck waddled to the sliding glass door and into her bedroom. As she closed the draperies, she didn't notice a figure move back into the shadows of the Haverford property.

CHAPTER 19

June 25 - Monday night

He had been exploring the new construction. He made it a habit to walk through any of the new building projects. It was amazing what could be accomplished when so much money was available. The house, after only one month, was completely framed, drywall up, electrical and plumbing complete. The roof was shingled three days ago. The windows installed and the exterior shakes and stonework being put on. There would be a lot to learn from this house. The Haverford kids were movers and shakers in New York City. He would have to wait until just before they moved in to set up the surveillance.

Getting into the Goldberg's home prior to Memorial Day had been easy. Living right next door, he could see them come and go. From his upstairs deck he could look below right into the shower and see where they hid the key. He had enjoyed watching his lovely neighbor shower, her not him.

They always came down early in the summer and he had timed it perfectly. The malware was installed on the laptop in the study and discreet bugs had been placed throughout the house. They weren't the only one. He had at least thirty houses in Loveladies under 'surveillance'. The amount of information he was obtaining was obscene.

He would continue to scout out more as the summer wore on. The local membership directories provided the names and addresses, all he had to do was research who they were and find out how to enter their home without witnesses or detection.

What did worry him was the nosy neighbor. What in the hell was she doing? Was she secretly stealing from her friend? He didn't see her leave with anything other than the bag with a towel. He would have to keep a very close eye on her. However, that dog was problematic. He would have to find a way to monitor her house.

He returned to his house and unlocked the door to his secret room. His wife was forbidden to enter it. She had no idea of his true mission, only that he worked for a special group-a kind of think tank he told her. Their purpose was to solve some of the most critical issues of the world. She was so proud of him.

He didn't tell her the true name or nature of the think tank or its connections with Vladimir Putin and the Kremlin. Most recently, they had been working on influencing the election of a candidate here in the United States that would not take a hard line with Russia. When they thought Hillary Clinton would win, they had to switch tactics toward voter fraud and attacks on her reputation. They had been successful influencing the election in the Ukraine and were confident now they would do the same with the United States Presidential election. With Trump winning, they began to devise ways to further divide the country, create chaos and destabilize the economic environment.

His mission had been a continuation of the Silvermaster and Ullmann agenda, while moving the intelligence gathered more toward key sectors that when hacked and taken over, could cause the United States to crumble.

Thankfully, his wife was not that smart. It had been an arranged marriage many years ago. She had come from Belarus to join him and was more than happy to do what he said in exchange for food, clothing, heat, and even air conditioning. She had grown up in horrible conditions, so she would do anything he asked of her.

Initially, she was a timid, pale and petite woman. Over the years, she became more capable in the kitchen and was companionable, which he needed more than love. After all, his mission was all his life really needed.

Even though they didn't live in one of the million dollar homes, theirs was comfortable enough. He didn't bother her, and she didn't bother him. He could come and go as he pleased, which was essential for the completion of his mission. She was basically there for cover, to clean the house, and cook what meals they ate together.

This room had been specially designed to be 'hidden' within the house. Anyone coming into their home would never suspect the back of the coat closet opened up into his office. Five large computer monitors were arranged on a custom desk built into two of the walls. Along the other walls were cabinets that housed the rest of his gear- listening devices, memory sticks, servers, special water tight canisters, GPS tracking devices and an assortment of lethal chemicals to be used only under special circumstances.

Over the years, Alek had obtained a number of chemicals, poisons and illicit drugs to be used as needed. He had been instructed to use whatever he needed to accomplish his goals. Since he was stationed at the shore, Saxitoxin was the most logical of poisons to use as it would be assumed a death was caused by shellfish.

Alek had been dormant for decades biding his time, creating the cover as a researcher working for a think tank. He and his wife tried to fit in with the residents of Loveladies, where he helped build many of the original houses in the 1950s with Silvermaster and Ullmann. Then his mentors died; Silvermaster in 1964 and Ullmann in 1993.

He had been recently reactivated by Russia; his primary mission was to locate people high up in the corporate, financial, and technical world and gain access to their company systems. Hackers could use this access to create alternative programs which they alone could control, effectively disabling any interference. In addition, the hackers would mimic the owner, sending out emails to their customers, contractors, subcontractors and any other company they did business with. From there, they would upload malicious files and launch programs that could do a number of things, like gain access to more sensitive information within the systems. If anyone receiving the fake email questioned it online, the hackers would impersonate the individual and tell them it was real. The hackers would gain access when the person clicked on the link, or went on a particular website where their username and passwords would give them access to more secure systems. It was ingenious how they moved through gaining access exponentially. This process was a bit different than what they had done in the past few years.

He knew just enough to complete his end of the mission. What he didn't know he learned on the internet. He really didn't understand what the hackers did. Coding, that was something really foreign to him. But what they accomplished in the Ukraine was marvelous. It amazed him that they could develop a code that when uploaded into someone's computer could do so much damage. Now, they were basically doing the same thing but he was installing the malware instead of using phishing email. They had to change up the method because people were getting more sophisticated and wary about what they opened in their email or what sites they visited. Norton and McAfee were on top of most threats, alerting and taking care of things. With the new software he installed, not only did the hackers have access to the company information, they could disable the security systems on the device.

Since he and his wife lived in Loveladies year around, he was able to break into most of the homes during the winter and install listening devices. When he was sure they had computers or laptops in the home, he would break in again if needed and install the spyware. He had been working on this for months accumulating more and more households.

Tomorrow morning he had to deliver the new data he had collected for this week. It would include any additional laptops he added and their programs, emails, logins, and passwords used on the computers. Once the hackers got the information, they would be able to link from that person's systems at the shore to their home, their office, phones and any and all of their contacts.

But first he would need to download whatever new information was available onto the special storage devices which would take about an hour or so. He could just upload it to the hackers, but it was decided that this additional layer of security was needed. Once they had access and the coding set up, they would disable the malware so it was undetectable.

While this went on, he would pack his lunch and beer in the cooler and store it on his boat. He would leave, as he normally did at six the next morning and make the drop at the designated coordinates that was fed daily into his GPS transponder, returning home at five with fresh fish for dinner.

His secondary mission was to prepare for the decommission of the Oyster Creek Generating Station in Forked River. There were a number of different scenarios that could take place and he would need to be ready for any of them. Regardless who managed the process; it was the storing and later the transportation of the highly radioactive fuel assemblies he was interested in. He would have to stay alert to the timeline the Exelon executive had posted regarding the shutdown.

Apparently, Exelon was moving up their timeline to close the Oyster Creek plant. Originally, it had been scheduled for October, now it would be mid-September. They would be implementing a method called SAFSTOR, which stood for safe storage, and using the sixty year Nuclear Regulatory rule for decommissioning the plant. They believed that this would be the most cost effective, safe, and environmentally friendly timeline. Alek was pleased to see that by shutting down Oyster Creek, the report noted that algae blooms would diminish; fish would increase in numbers and basically renew the ecosystem in Barnegat Bay. He truly enjoyed his fishing.

It was interesting that the environmentalists had issues with this. It seemed they were more concerned about the storing and cooling of the spent fuel rods in large tanks of water. With rising sea levels due to climate change and increasing numbers of hurricanes and storms in this area, they were worried a storm surge could be disastrous, damaging these tanks and thus releasing large amounts of radiation.

CHAPTER 20

June 27 - Wednesday

Wednesday, Miranda and the kids had to go home for the day. It was time for their dental hygiene visits and Kevin had an internship interview. Miranda didn't know too much about it just that it was in conjunction with course work. Maynard had to come home too, he wouldn't be able to stay at the shore house alone for the eight or so hours they would be away. It would be a busy day, but they should be back at the shore by ten that night.

The kids were up early and took Maynard out to do his morning business before breakfast. Miranda opened the screen door and reminded the kids to lock the shed before they left for the day. She saw Alek and his wife in their garden and waved hello.

They were on the road by eight thirty and thankfully, traffic was very light. This gave Miranda the opportunity to quiz Kevin about the internship and what it might entail.

"So, Kevin, you kind of sprung this on Dad and me. We had no idea you were considering an internship this semester. When does it start, who is it with, and what will you be doing?"

Kevin was in the back seat with Maynard and Miranda couldn't see his face. She imagined he would look a bit sheepish at the question. He knew better than to spring things on his parents with short notice.

"Mom, I just found out about the internship the school was offering this semester. There was only one for Finance majors so I thought I would apply. I only got the email a few days ago and I was glad I could schedule it around our trip back home."

"I know they only have several openings in a number of locations and the school offers other classes wherever they are so I can get the sixteen semester credits I need. That's all I know. My interview is in Florham Park."

Miranda sighed, "Well, please let Dad and I know all the details as soon as you get them so we can help you get ready."

They dropped the dog off at home; he would be alright for the few hours they would be at the dentist. Kevin would take the car to his interview after they returned home.

As Miranda was sitting in the dentist's office waiting for the kids to finish, she began planning for the Fourth of July which was the following Wednesday. Some of the kids' college friends would be coming for the party and staying over for a few days. She would have to get the meals planned, shopping done and all the beds and bathrooms ready for company. The Goldbergs would be joining them for the pre-party cookouts. She hoped they wouldn't be mad at her for creeping around their house while they weren't there.

CHAPTER 21

June 27 - Wednesday

The drop off yesterday was successful. He hadn't gone fishing today and was spending time with his wife. She had suggested they check the garden for any ripe vegetables for their dinner later that night.

That Craig woman told him everything he needed to know. It really was funny how well sound traveled on the lagoon! They would be gone for the day with the dog. This was the opportunity he had been waiting for, to find out what she was up to, and possibly gain access to the husband's business.

He thought about the best way to enter their house and decided it would be through the sliding glass doors by the rear of their pool. He could masquerade as one of the million pool cleaners on the island. He would inspect the pool; adding chemicals and skimming the bugs and leaves out. His wife wouldn't be able to see him at this angle and he knew the Goldbergs weren't home. The construction workers wouldn't pay him any attention. It wouldn't be too hard to pop the sliders, they were old. Maybe he would be lucky and one of the doors would be unlocked.

He waited an hour then told his wife he would be out running some errands. He would stop off at a pool supply store, then Target for a hat with a wide brim to make his deception complete. He already had his surveillance gear in the car so he should be done by lunch time. By tonight, he would be able to monitor everything that went on in that house.

CHAPTER 22

July 2 - Monday

The following Monday, Liz returned to the shore and found the outdoor porch light shattered to pieces. She called Miranda immediately, "Miranda, come over here quickly if you can. Something has happened and I am a bit nervous going into the house alone." Before Miranda could respond Liz hung up.

Climbing out of her car with a broom and dust pan, Miranda began her apology. "Liz, I have to beg your forgiveness. I did something and I hope you won't hate me for it. Let me clean up this mess for you to start with."

"Miranda, did you break our light?"

"Yes, but I can explain. Let me throw this glass away and I will tell you everything."

Liz sat on the steps with her mouth wide open as Miranda outlined exactly what she did last Monday night.

"Well, you know what they say; the road to Hell is paved with good intentions. I can understand how you would want to prove how easy it is to get into shore houses on the lagoons, but to go so far as to break our light? Richard will be livid!"

"Liz, I promise I will replace it and pay for the electrician. It really was necessary so that no one would see me."

"Well, you can explain it all to Richard when he gets here. He decided to take the week off for the Fourth of July holiday and he should be arriving any minute."

Miranda explained everything again to an annoyed Richard the minute he got out of his car. He admitted that her escapade did have some merit but he was still unhappy with the outcome. "Liz told me about that FBI/malware article. I haven't had this laptop checked in a while so I think it would be a good idea to have someone come in," Robert conceded.

They walked into the back room where Robert kept his laptop. Liz said, "Now this room really gives me the creeps. Let's get the cars unloaded, finish cleaning up this mess then decide what to do."

Outside, Liz said, "Over Memorial Day weekend I noticed that a few things seemed off in the office. I couldn't put my finger on it at the time; the room just looked different for some reason. I had forgotten to mention it to you because it was just an odd feeling."

Joining them, Richard said, "Well, that cinches it, I am going to call my IT guru to come out today or tomorrow and do a thorough scan of the laptop just to be sure. I can't take any chances of someone getting access to this proprietary information." Richard pulled out his cell phone to call his contact and schedule an appointment.

Later that afternoon, Liz called Miranda and invited her to Kubel's for Happy Hour. It was an older restaurant/bar in Barnegat Light that was a favorite of theirs. They placed their orders for martinis and scooped bowls of fresh, hot popcorn from the popper in the corner of the bar.

Miranda asked, "Are you guys still mad at me?"

Liz took a long drink of her martini and whispered, "Miranda, Richard's technician Bill came around eleven today. He handles security for many of the top firms in Philadelphia. Richard's laptop had some program installed that copied everything that was on the computer. Passwords, emails, spreadsheets, you name it. It was programmed to submit the information through a complex routing system to a specified encrypted IP address. He thinks whoever it is has a proxy server that would conceal his IP address. There was no way Bill could trace it. In addition, he found our landline was bugged and other listening devices scattered about the house. He wasn't sure what we should do so we have to be very careful what we say and do. He is coming to your house tomorrow to check your laptop and phones."

"I don't know what is going on, but until we find out, be quiet and shut down everything. Call Jack from some obscure phone and suggest he have his work computers checked out. We need to contact someone about this if your house is compromised also. If it is just our house, then it might be related to Richard's work. If you are involved too, then we have a much bigger problem."

Miranda thought for a minute then said, "Remember that guy we met at the Loveladies Harbor Organization picnic? His name is John Franklin. He lives one street over on the corner. He used to be a secret service agent for Obama. Maybe he can help?"

Before they left Kubel's, Miranda borrowed the bartender's cell phone and called Jack. She told him what she had done at the Goldberg's house, Richard's IT specialist uncovering spyware and the fact that they too, could be bugged. Jack assured her that whatever was found in their home would be taken care of. He asked that she contact him tomorrow after Bill did his "sweep" of their house and equipment.

Keslie Patch-Bohrod

CHAPTER 23

July 3 - Tuesday

Miranda woke up in a panic. Their big Fourth of July party was tomorrow, a bunch of kids would be arriving soon, Bill was coming to search for bugs and she had to straighten the house, prepare meals and remain calm. Impossible!

One thing was for certain, she couldn't do it alone. Erica and Kevin were put in charge of readying the house for their guests and cousins. They had to make sure there were enough places for everyone to sleep such as couches, beds or single mattresses that could fit on the floor. Jack's brother and sister had the other bedrooms. Miranda's brother and family couldn't attend so they had plans to see them over Christmas break in Florida.

Tonight's dinner would have to be simple. Hot dogs, hamburgers, corn and oven roasted potatoes. Liz was bringing a salad and dessert. The beer keg was being delivered soon and Kevin promised to ice it so they could start drinking it tonight. Now that both kids and their friends were twenty-one, it seemed that was all they cared about. Miranda would remind Jack he would have to talk to all the kids about responsible drinking and not to get too rowdy and disturb the other neighbors. Most importantly, they could not leave the property if they had been drinking.

Jack had changed his mind and come down to the shore last night after their phone call. He was planning to be down the rest of the week, but had hoped to get in half a day's work Tuesday. With the news Miranda dropped on him, he knew he had to be there when Bill arrived.

When the doorbell rang, everyone stopped what they were doing. Miranda made the 'shushing' sign by putting her index finger up to her lips. They all knew they couldn't say anything while Bill was doing his work. Jack opened the door, shook Bill's hand and showed him to the back bedroom desk where all their electronics were. Bill set down his briefcase, pulled out the chair, sat and picked up the first phone. Jack left him, returning a few minutes later to deliver him a cup of coffee. Bill smiled, mouthed "Thank you" and returned to his work.

An hour and a half later, Bill came out of the back room with a device in his hand. He began a systematic scanning of each of the rooms. When he was done with the entire house, Bill motioned for the entire family to meet him in the back bathroom where he shut the door.

He began in a whisper, "This room is clear but I have found a number of recording devices throughout your house, and I am not sure I found everything. I will show you where each one is located, just so you know. You have the same strange software on your laptop Miranda that I found on Richard's but nothing on the phones or the kids' electronics; possibly, because they always have their phones and iPads with them. Jack, your stuff is clean. We need to talk about how we will proceed. Miranda, Liz told me you might have a contact with the FBI or something?"

"Yes, we met an ex-secret service agent who lives on the next street over. Jack is quite friendly with him. I think he might be able to refer us to someone if he can't help us directly. I don't think the local police are up to this type of issue. Should I have Jack walk over there and see if he is home?"

"I think that would be a good idea. If he is, I suggest we talk with him over there."

A few minutes later, Jack came back and joined everyone in bathroom. He reported neither John nor his wife were at home. He left a note in their mailbox asking John to call him on his cell phone when he got in, saying it was an urgent, confidential matter.

Bill took a deep breath, blew it out and said, "In the meantime, I am going to ask you to do something that might be a bit difficult. I had to ask the Goldbergs to do the same thing. You have to act like you don't know your house is bugged. We can't let them, whoever they are, know we know about them. Not until we have the FBI or some other law enforcement agency involved. They might want to set up a sting type operation which I am sure will take some time to set up. So let me take you around and show you where everything is."

Bill walked them from room to room pointing to the various hiding places, such as the headboards in the bedrooms, behind the couches and under the kitchen cabinets.

"Remember to go about your normal activities, but don't discuss business or anything important. We don't know what they are after. If we just remove the stuff, they could just reinstall it or get into someone else's home. Call me as soon as you hear from John, but do so from Jack's phone somewhere safe, maybe from the beach. The sound of the surf would help hide some of the conversation from listening ears. I haven't checked your cars, so please be aware they might not be safe either."

Bill gathered up his tools and devices and left their home. The Craig's went about their business of getting ready for the onslaught of guests.

The evening was filled with eating, drinking and laughing. College students will be college students. They drank beer, played beer pong in the pool and listened to rap music. Jack had to tell them more than once to keep it down. Finally, the adults moved inside the house, leaving the kids outside to have their fun. It was so difficult not to talk about what had happened.

Liz had just gotten the dessert out of the refrigerator when Jack's phone rang. He saw it was an unknown number and went out front to answer it. He came back in and wrote a note for everyone to read. JOHN IS HOME NOW AND WE CAN COME OVER AND TALK.

Miranda went outside and told the kids the adults were going to take a little walk and would be back in about a half an hour. Dessert was on the table and they should help themselves.

Keslie Patch-Bohrod

CHAPTER 24

July 3 - Tuesday

John and Lori Franklin lived on the corner of the next street. The Craigs met them last year at the Loveladies Harbor Organization picnic and got to know them at their last Fourth of July party. Jack always invited everyone he ran into when he was out on his walks. They had been very friendly and John had shared some very exciting stories of his life as a secret service agent. As they sat in their kitchen, John told them he was now working for a Sheriffs' office in Northern New Jersey.

Miranda began to tell John and Lori about Richard's IT specialist finding spyware and listening devices in their homes. She was reluctant to tell them what she and Liz had been researching fearing they would look foolish. Of course, Liz had to tell them about Miranda's night swim and breaking and entering.

John listened with great interest. He agreed with Bill's recommendation that the devices remain in place for the time being and suggested next steps. Arrangements would be made in the next day or two for the most appropriate law enforcement group to be notified to investigate. He would discuss this with his superiors and his contacts with the FBI and possibly Homeland Security. Without giving too much information, he led them to believe that this was not a complete surprise to him.

As they were leaving, Jack, of course, invited John and Lori to their Fourth of July party the next day. John accepted saying it would give him an opportunity to take a look around and talk with some of the other neighbors. Maybe someone else would mention computer problems. Miranda remembered the conversation she and Jack had with the two couples at Daymark and gave John their name and addresses.

Walking back to the house, Miranda pulled Liz away from their husbands. "Liz, tomorrow at the party, let's try to get more information about our neighbors like what they do, where they work, and where they are from."

Liz nodded her head, "Especially Frederick. I will try to sit down with him and try to get him to really open up. Do you think Alek and his wife will show up?"

"No, they never come to our parties."

CHAPTER 25

July 4 - Wednesday

Miranda woke up at six when Maynard stuck his wet nose in her face. Time for breakfast and a quick morning walk. After she put food in his bowl, she got herself dressed and put some instant coffee in a to-go cup. The kids would sleep until at least ten o'clock and Jack would be up in a few minutes. He would make a pot of coffee and put on the business channel to see what the market was doing in other parts of the world since the New York Stock Exchange was closed for the holiday.

Miranda and Maynard left the house and walked up their street to the main thoroughfare, Long Beach Boulevard. At this time of day, it was very quiet. There was a bit of mist coming off the ocean, but Miranda could tell it was going to be a very hot day. They were going to need to put up all the patio umbrellas and the tent so their guests could have shade. She was thankful for the quiet; it would allow her to create a to-do list in her head for the party. The friends and relatives that weren't already on the island would arrive early to avoid the traffic.

Breakfast/brunch items would need to be out for people to snack on until the catered food arrived around one thirty. She had croissants, bagels, muffins, and fruit salad to start. Antonio would deliver the trays of hot and cold Italian food later and the guests usually would bring desserts. Jack told her the musician would arrive at one and play until four o'clock. There really wasn't much to do. Feeling somewhat relieved, she and Maynard made their way back to the house.

Since their guests would be coming and going through various doors, they worried Maynard might make an escape and they wouldn't be aware he was gone. So, Miranda had made arrangements with Lucky's Bed and Biscuit to pick him up and he would spend the day at the doggie resort and spa. He could run and play with the other dogs, swim in the pool, take a walk with one of the employees then have his lunch and a nap in the afternoon. They would even bring him back at the end of the day. It just made life easier for everyone and they wouldn't worry about him getting into the food or leaving hot, steaming, and fragrant mounds of poo in the backyard where the guests were walking and eating.

As expected the kids got up at ten, and guests began to arrive. Miranda didn't have any time to think about the bugs or computer tampering. She put out the trays of food and pots of coffee and tea. Liz and Richard arrived as did Jack's siblings and family. By noon, Miranda counted sixty-five people in the backyard. She had to mingle with her neighbors and friends and make sure everyone was having a good time.

Liz caught her as she was putting chilled white wines in the large ice bucket on the outdoor bar. "I just saw Frederick walk in. Should I take him a glass of wine? And what is his last name? I don't think you have ever mentioned that to me and frankly, I only pay attention to people's first names."

Miranda said, "No wine, I remember last year, he really liked the Blue Moon we had in the keg. Why don't you take him one in a red solo cup with a slice of orange? His last name is Wasserman, and remember it is Dr. Wasserman."

Miranda looked over to where Frederick was standing just inside the back gate. He looked so old and feeble; she wondered how he was able to stand on his own. When he began to walk further into her yard, he did so cautiously; he would take a step, balance his body, then take the next step. She couldn't imagine what it must be like to be that old or have the experiences he had over his ninety-two years.

Liz did as Miranda suggested and soon was sitting and chatting with Frederick. John and Lori arrived and they too began talking with the neighbors, John giving Miranda a wink.

Taking this as a cue to do the same, Miranda began to target and talk to the neighbors she knew little about. After an hour, she realized there was nothing mysterious about the people she spoke to. She glanced over at Liz and found she was still in deep conversation with Frederick. Liz must really be getting his life story.

At one o'clock, the steel drummer set up her instruments and began to play reggae music. It was a bit too loud to carry on a conversation, so people either began to dance or went for a swim in the pool. The kids took noodles from the shed and decided the lagoon was the better place to cool off and drink beer. Everyone seemed to be enjoying themselves. Except Alek. He was standing on his upper deck looking at the party. Miranda was worried he would call the police and complain about the noise. She called Jack over and suggested he again invite Alek and his wife to join them. As Jack moved to the far end of the dock to yell up to Alek, Alek moved back into his house.

Jack turned around to Miranda and shrugged his shoulders. "Hopefully, he won't complain about our noise. We can't be any noisier than the Haverford's construction or Stein's get-togethers. It would be a real shit show if both of them were competing with us today!" Luckily, the construction workers had taken the day off for the Fourth of July.

Antonio's always provided great food for the Craig's parties, partly because the Craig kids worked for him. But this year, he really outdid himself. Thankfully, Miranda had set up a number of long tables to hold all the warming catering trays, salads, and rolls when he arrived about one fifteen.

Erica and Kevin helped Antonio to uncover the cavatelli and broccoli, sausage and peppers, chicken and veal parmesan, baked ziti, vegetable lasagna, shrimp scampi and an incredible looking seafood marinara. Next came the platters of grilled vegetables and baskets of fresh Italian bread. The trays of Italian cookies, cheesecake squares and freshly filled cannolis were taken inside to be out of the direct sunlight and heat of the afternoon. These would be brought out later.

Even before they were done setting up, people began lining up with their paper plates. Thankfully, Miranda had planned to serve about this time and had asked Antonio to make sure the food was hot when delivered. She guessed some people were never taught manners and wouldn't wait until they were invited to begin to serve themselves.

Everyone seemed to be enjoying themselves, making repeated trips to the food tables. There was more than enough food and hopefully, they would have some leftovers for tomorrow.

A few hours later, Liz grabbed Miranda and took her out the front door.

"I have so many details from Frederick, but I don't know what it all means. We will have to find a place tomorrow that is safe to talk and decide what information is pertinent to share with John's contacts."

Miranda replied, "That sounds like a good idea. By the way, did you see Alek on the balcony staring at us? Jack tried to invite him over, but he just went inside. Strange! Let's try to get together tomorrow at some point."

By seven thirty that night, the food, what was left of it, was put in the refrigerator, the music was over and people were exhausted. No one seemed to care about fireworks. Jack's family had moved inside to begin to take showers and get ready to chill for the rest of the night. The kids were talking about showering and taking the LBI shuttle to a club down at the other end of the island. Oh, to be young again.

The last of the neighbors were leaving, John and Lori among them. John shook Jack's hand and said, "I will call you tomorrow about fishing. Maybe Richard would like to come with us."

Jack understood what John was implying. "I will let Richard know. I am sure he would love to join us. Maybe the wives want to come too."

Finally, a very tired Maynard was dropped off. After making a stop in the backyard to check out all the new smells and to see if there were any leftovers or crumbs scattered about, he immediately went to his dog bed in the corner and went to sleep.

CHAPTER 26

July 4 - Wednesday

Frederick left the Craig's party after having spent a few hours enjoying himself. He had a chance to meet and talk with some of his neighbors and enjoy good food and drink. The Craigs always tried to include everyone and made the afternoon an enjoyable one. He especially liked his conversation with Liz Goldberg. She was such a lovely woman. They had talked religion, the war, and the problems the Jews had getting on with their lives. He probably shouldn't have told her so much about himself, but being ninety-two years old, what would it matter.

What could they do to him now, kill him? Ha. That would be a relief. He had been working with Chicky and the CIA since coming to America. It had been a condition of his relocation and licensing. He knew several countries were helping Nazis' escape their crimes by working with their security forces against the Soviets. He kept telling himself that he must continue to play the part of a European Jew who wanted a better life and to help others. Using his career as a psychiatrist to uncover spies was a way to do this. The Cold War was a frightening time for everyone and it required unique methods. But what really amazed him was that the Cold War never really ended. Just the tactics changed. The stakes were even higher now.

He recalled, in the early days of the 1950s and 1960s, he and some of his fellow psychiatrists were involved in various programs funded by the CIA to create psychological warfare techniques. He had been part of the research that was conducted when he was on staff at the hospital.

The use of LSD, sleep deprivation and electroshock therapy as interrogation methods was very intriguing to him. But, he refused to be part of the programs where prisoners or cancer patients were exposed to biological weapons. He had to draw the line somewhere, feeling he would be no better than the world he fled from. Although, he confessed to himself, much of what he had done had been the price he had to pay for his freedom and his new life.

After Project MKUltra was exposed to the public in 1975, he feared their efforts would all come to a grinding stop and he would be exposed. The CIA had been experimenting with drugs and techniques on subjects to get confessions. It was all about mind control. It started in 1953 and was said to have ended in 1973. The scientists used LSD, hypnosis and other methods. It was wild what they were doing. Thankfully, he had been a 'bit player' and little attention had been paid to him.

It was such a beautiful evening. The temperature was a perfect sixty-seven degrees with a light, fragrant breeze. Frederick opened windows in his bedroom, kitchen and living room to let in as much of the clean air as possible. It would make work a bit more enjoyable.

He sat down in his favorite chair and pulled his briefcase onto his lap. Sorting through the ten files he brought with him, he selected one and pulled it out. He reached in the outside flap of his case and removed his Dictaphone. His colleagues mocked him, saying he needed to change with the times and get a computer. He found it so much easier to speak his thoughts rather than take the time to write them down. His reports were much more complete and he didn't lose his train of thought because his typing couldn't keep up. Plus, with the arthritis in his hands, he found it much too difficult to write but a few scribbled notes. Thankfully, he had a trusted transcription service that Chicky recommended. Frederick didn't like to keep copies of his reports, he knew what they were doing would alarm the American public and he didn't want to be caught with evidence that might convict him of a crime. The reports he gave to Chicky were coded to some degree and he was never named in the reports. They were mainly interested in the information he was able to extract from the patients.

Most of the Capitol insiders that he saw right now had information pertaining to the current President and certain Pentagon employees. Chicky would forward these reports to the necessary agency. Currently, there were three patients that were providing some leads to Soviet spies along the East Coast. Their superiors had made the psychiatric evaluations a necessity of their employment. Employees needed a clean bill of health not only physically but mentally.

For these patients targeted by the CIA, he had to be especially careful not to give anything away. He had to move slowly, developing the rapport necessary to move onto the next critical steps that led to interrogation. Sometimes that meant he would have to sit through hours of sessions, listening to these people ramble on about their childhood or spouse or maybe even problems with fellow employees. He wasn't a classically trained Freudian psychiatrist; there was no couch to hide behind. He sat face to face with his patients and fought to stay awake.

Although he wasn't part of the CIA's mind control program or the interrogation of prisoners, he was part of a special ops group that used some of the mind control techniques on select patients with suspected ties to the Soviet Union.

He hoped in the next few appointments to convince these patients to try mild sedation and hypnosis to help them break through their defenses. He would explain the benefits in terms of uncovering fear and help change unwanted behavior and perceptions. It was all a bunch of hooey and psychobabble, but if he said it with enough conviction, they might believe him. If they didn't, he would sneak drugs into their water or coffee. He was pragmatic; he had to get information one way or another.

Regardless of their consent, it gave him a chance to utilize those techniques developed through Project MKUltra. He had found LSD and hypnosis quite beneficial in getting the information they were looking for. Not only that, he could impart hypnotic suggestions and instructions to use at a later time.

Last summer, before his dreadful accident, thought Frederick, Chicky had suggested he renew his efforts with his friend in Loveladies. Their suspicions had increased to the point where evidence had to be found quickly. Frederick would have to invite his friend over and lace his tea with LSD and attempt to hypnotize him in an effort to uncover what he was up to. With Chicky dead and no one else providing guidance at this time, he knew he had to take action.

The rest of his normal patients, those not targeted by the CIA, were employed in a number of different settings. One was a defense contractor, another worked for the Pennsylvania Public Utilities Commission in the IT department. Some were even CEOs of major corporations in Pennsylvania, New Jersey and Washington, D.C. He had severely reduced his caseload over the last year due to his advanced age. He couldn't keep up the workload and was just too tired anymore. Soon it would be time to completely retire and with Chicky dead, sooner would be better than later.

As he began to dictate his first report, there was a knock on his front door. It was very dark out now and he wondered who was coming to visit him.

Frederick opened the door and with a big smile says, "My dear friend, to what do I owe the pleasure?"

"I just wanted to see how you were getting on. I wasn't able to go the Craig's party; I had some work that needed to be done in the house. The toilet was constantly running and it was driving my wife crazy. So I had to run to Home Depot and get a repair kit. So how was it? Who was there?" asked Alek Pronin.

"It was quite nice as always, they are charming hosts. They had some wonderful shellfish pasta and I think I ate a bit too much of it. I don't often have the opportunity to eat that kind of food. You know me, usually, I eat like a bird. Today, I ate like a pig! I spent a bit of time with your next door neighbor, Liz Goldberg. You really should be friendlier with our neighbors. It is good to be social."

Alek scowled, "I like to pick my friends. Besides, they are in a different age group and I find it hard to relate to them. I prefer people like you Frederick. We enjoy our tea, our conversation and a good smoke. And with smoking being taboo now, I can't find any place acceptable to light up except at your house!"

Frederick jumped up out of his chair and said, "Oh my, what horrible manners I have! Tea! I will be right back." He left the room and went into the kitchen to put the kettle on and prepared tea and some cookies for his guest.

What an opportunity, thought Frederick. *He is here and won't suspect anything!* Frederick removed the LSD from the pocket of his lab coat hanging by the back door. He had come directly to the shore from work.

When the water boiled, he put the LSD in the bottom of Alek's cup, adding the tea bag and hot water. He had selected a very strong flavor of tea, one that had a bitter taste to it to help hide the taste of the LSD. Alek had had this tea before so he shouldn't notice anything different. The pure liquid form he was using would be very strong, so he only used a few micrograms. In addition, he had to add an antipsychotic to counteract some of the effects of the LSD. He had been experimenting with a number of different drugs over the years and finally came up with clozapine, an older drug. He found that in combination with the LSD, the patient would have better cognitive function, thus giving him more accurate information. The purpose of these studies within Project MKUltra had been to develop a truth serum, but early on it was very unpredictable. He had continued to develop a number of different drug combinations in hopes of finding one that met their needs. The one he would use tonight was just that combination. It also lessened the chances of suicidal thought but did make the patient very drowsy and sleepy. He finished setting up the tray.

While Frederick was in the kitchen, Alek pulled out a pack of cigarettes. He carefully removed three and inserted them into Frederick's pack, so that when he pulled one out, he would get one laced with the chemical. He had been watching the party to see what food was offered. He saw the array of seafood and noticed Frederick eating a plate of it. This was a perfect opportunity to use the Saxitoxin. He had soaked some of the tobacco in it for the cigarettes and it would cause death mimicking paralytic shellfish poisoning, being more toxic inhaled. It was a toxin that was produced by algae and it contaminated scallops, oysters, mussels, and clams. When he died, it would be assumed it was because of his advanced age and tainted seafood at the Craig's. He hurried to unplug the landline and hid Frederick's cellphone he saw sitting on the side table by the couch. It would ruin things if Frederick was able to call for help.

Frederick returned with the tea and cookies. They sat together and talked about the weather, work, and politics. Alek commented how much he enjoyed this tea and remembered Frederick had served it the last time he was over.

They had been chatting for about thirty minutes when Alek began to notice everything seemed to be more colorful, sharper. He could hear the wind passing through the curtains. It seemed to be getting terribly warm in the room, and he asked Frederick if more windows could be opened.

Frederick got up and opened the door to the outdoor porch. He returned to his chair and tea and began to ask Alek a few questions about his fishing. He knew Alek was ready for more in-depth interrogation when he admitted to buying fish at Viking Village Fish Market to fool his wife about his daily activities.

Grabbing his Dictaphone, Frederick hit the record button to begin the questioning.

"Alek, please tell me about the purposes of your fishing trips. Where do you go, what do you do?"

"I deliver data to specific locations in the Atlantic Ocean."

"Please tell me more Alek. How long have you been doing this and where do you get the data?"

"I began to collect the data about two years ago, installing a special spyware on computers throughout Loveladies."

"Alek, who do you give the data to?"

"Hackers working for the Russians."

Frederick couldn't believe his luck. He had to think what he wanted to know and ask his questions succinctly otherwise Alek might give confusing or false information. He paused and picked up his cigarettes.

Tapping one out of the pack, he said, "What is the purpose of the hackers?"

As Alek started to reply, Frederick lit his cigarette and took a long, deep inhale of smoke.

"To disrupt the American economy."

There were enough toxins in the first few inhales to insure Frederick's death in very short period of time, inhalation sped up the effects. He would experience a number of unpleasant symptoms with the final being respiratory failure.

Frederick took another drag from his cigarette and asked, "Alek, what is your timeline for this disruption?"

Alek was starting to show signs of anxiety. Frederick suggested he too have a cigarette. As he waited for Alek to light his own, he finished his.

Almost immediately, Frederick began to lick his lips and rub his fingers together. He tried to stand up but his legs went out from under him, he could barely move his muscles in his arms and legs. Unable to move, but fully aware, he stared at Alek.

Still experiencing a distortion in reality, Alek just sat there, watched and smoked his cigarette as his friend died. He noted his lack of movement and the thin trail of smoke from his stubbed out cigarette in the ashtray. A nice cool breeze came in through the windows and he yawned. Picking up a cookie and eating it he wondered what he should do. Maybe take a little nap before cleaning up in here.

The couch looked very inviting, so he took off his shoes, moved the pillow onto the cushions and lay down. Soon he was fast asleep and without a care in the world.

CHAPTER 27

July 5 – Thursday

The early morning sounds of seagulls assaulted his senses and he abruptly sat up on the couch. Looking around, panic struck. What the hell happened here? What happened to me, what did I do?

He got up and looked around and found Frederick dead, lying on the ground in front of his chair. It all came rushing back to him what had happened the previous night. The tea, cookies, cigarettes and conversation. Oh god, what did I tell him? The Dictaphone was next to Frederick's chair. Alek picked it up and put it in his pocket.

Then he picked up his cup and saucer, which was empty but had his DNA and fingerprints on it so he went to the kitchen to wash and dry them. Careful not to touch after cleaning, he used the dish towel to put them away in the cupboards. He used the towel to wipe the chair, coffee table, couch, cigarette pack and door knob. He removed the files from Frederick's briefcase and the one he had laid on the coffee table. The listening devices in the living room and bedroom were the next to go. As he left Frederick's house, he remembered the ash tray and pack of cigarettes. He emptied the ashtray into the dish towel and carefully removed the other two cigarettes he had put in Frederick's pack. He paused a moment to remember his movements to make sure he had not missed anything. He locked and closed the door behind him.

The Craig's backyard was empty. Everyone was still asleep inside; hopefully sound asleep after all the booze they drank the day before. He would have to be extra quiet so the dog didn't wake up and start barking at him. It was early enough in the morning that he could crawl through the back yard and into the lagoon, swimming directly across to his dock and onto his property. It didn't matter if the files got wet, he would be destroying them anyway. Hopefully, no one would find Frederick for several days. He carefully disposed of the towel and cigarettes into an old milk carton and stuffed it into the bottom of the garbage can. He would have to remember to take this out later before he left to go fishing. Tomorrow was trash pickup day.

With any luck, the CIA would be implicated in the death of Frederick, should they somehow stumble on the chemical. Saxitoxin was a known military and CIA chemical weapon that was supposed to be destroyed years ago but the CIA kept a bit of it in its bag of tricks. It would be assumed Frederick was an escaped World War II Nazi used by the CIC/CIA during the Cold War to spy on the Soviets. Alek was well aware of his path in getting to the United States. His death might have been their way of covering their tracks. Chicky's death would also add to this scenario; cleaning house to remove any trace.

Alek had known it was only a matter of time before Frederick and Chicky would have been able to implicate him. He had been monitoring Frederick for years. He had even visited him at his other home and office, leaving discreet listening devices there too. What surprised Alek was how the two of them had managed to find people that would eventually lead them to him. Regardless, the hackers had access to each one of his patients and all of their contacts as well.

Late last summer he had overheard Frederick and Chicky talking on Frederick's back porch. People really needed to be more aware how sound carries on the lagoon, thought Alek. He was able to hear every word they said even though they thought they were trying to be discreet. Chicky was pushing Frederick to make headway with several patients, naming them. These were people affiliated with the think tank. Alek immediately knew he had to terminate Chicky and eventually, Frederick.

He saw his chance when the Craigs began packing up last Labor Day. He could hear them talking with the Goldbergs across the lagoon. They had to take one of the kids back to school and would see Liz and Richard next summer. That meant the dog would go too.

Watching from his roof top deck, he saw them back out onto their street and head toward the boulevard. Quickly he ran downstairs and out to the end of his dock, taking cover by his evergreen trees that grew on the sides of his property. Everyone seemed to be inside enjoying their breakfast, a cup of coffee or sleeping in. He eased himself into the water by his tree line, and waited until he saw Chicky dive into the lagoon for his morning swim.

Alek had maintained his strong, muscular physique even after he stopped working construction in the late 1960s. At some point, he thought, strength would be needed in his job. Will this be the first of many opportunities to support his continued exercise? He had to do something on his boat out in the ocean. Luckily, his boat was big enough to allow his 6 foot frame to do his three hundred daily push-ups.

As his habit, Chicky would swim to the end of the lagoon by the bay entrance, return, swimming to the other end, then home. He passed by Alek, but didn't see him as he hid under his dock. Slowly and quietly, Alek breast stroked after him until he caught up by Chicky's boat. Alek was much stronger than Chicky and a bit younger, so it was easy for him to pull him under. There was not much of a struggle, as Alek grabbed some of the line from Chicky's boat and wrapped it around his torso and limbs. He tried to make it look like Chicky got caught up and struggled, eventually losing the battle and drowning.

After pushing Chicky's body under his boat, Alek slowly breast stroked back to his dock and quickly got out and went inside.

About an hour later, he heard some shouts and went outside to see what was going on. He saw one of the Haverford kids yelling as he was trying to pull his father out of the water. Someone was yelling to 'Call 911' as other neighbors came out to see what was going on. He smiled to himself and walked back into his house.

Later that day, the police arrived to question the neighborhood.

When they stopped at his house, he had already showered and put on dry clothes. They asked what he had been doing all day and if he had seen anything. Of course, he had been home all day and had not seen or heard anything. They took his statement and left.

At that time, it had been one down and one to go. Now the day after Fourth of July, Frederick was gone. Things were shaping up.

What he did not plan for or remember to check for, were traces of the laced tobacco that fell on the floor from the three cigarettes he placed in Frederick's pack or the few pieces left at the bottom of the pack. He also forgot to close the windows in the house. The body would be found a bit sooner than he anticipated.

As he walked around the side of his house, his thoughts went to his wife. *Oh my god, she is going to wonder what happened to me. Hopefully, she hasn't called the police to report me missing. Then I won't have an alibi for Frederick's murder.*

He went to the outdoor shower to the side of his house and stripped off his clothes. Thankfully, she always left a stack of towels on the bench inside. He turned on the cold water to help clear the cobwebs in his head and thought about what he would tell her. Finishing, he wrapped the towel around his waist and walked out toward the garden. She was just coming out of the house to do her weeding.

"Oh, there you are! Did you have some urgent project you had to finish? Your lights were on in your office and the door was locked. I called you for dinner last night but you never responded. Were you wearing headphones? No matter, there are leftovers in the refrigerator or I can make you some breakfast if you are hungry."

He was ravenous.

Had he forgotten to turn out the light? He must have. But first, he would eat something, dispose of the Dictaphone and files from Frederick's house, and then turn out the light in his office.

After his wife made him an omelet and coffee, he took the trash out, including his stash from Frederick's, except for the Dictaphone. He retrieved his dirty clothes from the shower, emptying the pockets before putting them in the laundry room.

Returning to his office, he noted that indeed the light was on and the door locked. Funny, he was always so careful. With what happened last night, it didn't surprise him that he could have forgotten to shut it off. He sat down at his desk and turned on the Dictaphone. He was shocked to hear his voice giving details of his mission. What had Frederick given him that would make him talk like that? Thankfully, he was able to clean the place out and now he would be able to destroy the recording device. This could have gotten so out of hand.

He put together a brief encrypted report of what had transpired over the last few days, selected the appropriate canister and went to pack his lunch and coffee for fishing. It was just about six in the morning.

Keslie Patch-Bohrod

CHAPTER 28

July 5 - Thursday

No one wanted to get up the next morning. Between the heat, food, alcohol and the long day, sleep was the only thing that mattered. That is, until Alek fired up his boat at six that morning and worked his two hundred horse power Yamaha motor into a smoking frenzy. Even with the windows closed and the air conditioning on, it was still loud and smelly.

Miranda remembered when Alek used to get up at five thirty every morning back in the early nineties to go fishing. Jack's parents owned the house then, and air conditioning hadn't been put in yet. With the windows open all night to catch any cool breeze, it was inevitable that any outside noise would wake everyone up. The entire family used to get so mad at him. Today, she thought he was getting back at them for the party noise yesterday.

Miranda got up and let Maynard out to do his business. She stood outside and watched as Alek's boat eventually left his dock and headed down the lagoon toward Barnegat Bay.

Everyone had been so helpful in cleaning up after the party; there wasn't much to be done. Miranda had some time to herself and decided she would head into Surf City to one of the coffee shop/internet cafes to look over the stack of articles Diane had printed for her. She could also access one of the computers if she needed to do further research while she was there, since her own laptop still had the malware on it.

After getting her hazelnut coffee and an everything bagel with vegetable cream cheese, she found a quiet corner armchair with a side table. It was still rather early and she had the place all to herself.

Miranda thought as she pulled out the first sheet of paper Diane printed, it was probably best if she got an overview of what she found. That way she would know if she needed her to do a bit more research.

The first was about a German submarine found off the coast of New Jersey in 1991. This one didn't seem that relevant to her query. Frederick didn't arrive in the United States by sub.

On the next page, Diane made a note about the FBI and CIA recruiting Nazi's in the hunt for Soviet spies during the 1950s and had actually assisted some to come to the U.S. Miranda made a note also; if Frederick was a Nazi, then Chicky being with an intelligence agency could have helped him to come to the U.S. and put him to work hunting communists. She wondered if Chicky was ever stationed in Europe or South America.

Miranda had found similar information in the book Diane gave her. It had amazed her that the Red Cross and Catholic Church had been involved with aiding in the Nazis' escape after the war. It documented their departure from European countries, but what interested Miranda most were those escaping through Austria and Italy to South America along what was called the 'Ratline'. She recalled that Frederick had originally come from Austria and had gone to school in Argentina. Her suspicions of him were growing.

The next bit of information Diane shared was about Johann Breyer who was almost ninety, had been arrested because he was believed to have been an SS guard at Auschwitz and Birkenau. He had joined the SS at the age of seventeen. The neighbors had been asked what they knew of Mr. Breyer and his past. No one was aware of what he had done and actually had nice things to say about him. Miranda thought to herself, *See! You never know who your neighbor really is!*

Other articles talked about the Most Wanted Nazi War Criminals, that having access to better health care, many war criminals could still be alive in their nineties. Again, that could be Frederick! Could U.S. Intelligence have been influential getting him licensed in the United States to allow him to practice in Philadelphia as a psychiatrist? Could he be working with the government in tracking Communists? Surely, there were many other psychiatrists in Loveladies and LBI.

Miranda also remembered reading about a married couple with two children living in Montclair, New Jersey. There were arrested by the FBI about ten years ago when they were able to prove them to be Russian spies. She also recalled how there was a TV show about a

124

spy couple. It was called *The Americans* and starred Keri Russell and Matthew Rhys.

The next was an old article from the 1940s. Nazi spies, chosen by the Gestapo because they looked Jewish, entered the Netherlands. They went to synagogues to learn as much as they could about Jewish services and were circumcised to complete their disguise. Later, they were captured, suspected of being spies and taken in for questioning. The authorities, being clever, asked a rabbi to examine the men. He found they were not circumcised according to Jewish tradition. They were arrested as Nazi spies. *Hmmm, maybe she could get Liz to check out Frederick,* snickered Miranda to herself.

A number of news stories included in the stack of information, referenced a Russian spy ship, the Viktor Leonov being seen around February 2017 very close to the Connecticut coast, another reported it close to New Jersey and another spotted it off the coast of Delaware. Miranda couldn't believe how close they were allowed to come to the East Coast.

The last web article was the most interesting of them all. The Ukraine had been under attack from Russian hackers around 2015. They had disrupted their elections and attacked the infrastructure, shutting down the power grids. What was most frightening was the premise that the hackers were practicing on the Ukraine. Practicing for what or whom? The United States?

Many people argued that our recent Presidential election had been tampered with. With our nation being severely divided and embittered, wouldn't chaos ensue if something happened to our power system or food supply? Is this the ultimate Russian weapon, Miranda thought. We would all kill each other over food and supplies. This would clear the way for immediate take over, just clean up the dead bodies and move right on in. Why use nuclear weapons which would make the land uninhabitable?

Miranda had a sick thought, '*Maybe I should go online right now to Costco.com and order a bunch of those Emergency food ARK one month supply kits. Even if we don't need it, it does have a twenty year shelf life.*'

CHAPTER 29

July 5 - Thursday

Miranda returned home to find everyone up and the kitchen a mess. The kids had decided to take all the food that remained from yesterday and heat it up for lunch. Jack was nowhere to be found. Since there were so many left-overs, she called the Goldbergs and the Franklins to join in the feeding frenzy. This would also give them a chance to plan the 'fishing trip' John had suggested at the party. They really needed a place and time for them to pool their information and make plans for the logical next steps. She felt certain Liz and John had insights into the neighbors after all the socializing yesterday.

Jack walked in with the Franklins, having been over there making plans for the next day's outing. The Goldbergs were eager to move forward and offered to supply the sandwiches and drinks for the boat trip. Jack promised to pick up the bait later in the day as they would be leaving about six the next morning.

Richard whispered, "We should try to leave shortly after Alek and follow him out to his fishing spot since he seems to have such luck catching fish day after day."

The friends and relatives had left shortly after lunch and it was a quiet afternoon until the sawing began. The Craigs, Goldbergs and Franklins spent the rest of the day eating, drinking the Blue Moon beer in the keg, what remained of it and hanging by the pool. They turned their music up a bit more and tried to make the best of it.

At five that afternoon, they all watched as Alek's boat made its way down the lagoon to his dock. He got off, grabbed the hose and began washing off the salt water from the fiberglass hull. Next he removed the fish from the live well and proceeded to clean it at his sink station on the dock. The head, spine and tail he threw to the circling seagulls. This act made Miranda and Jack furious. People weren't supposed to feed the gulls. Once, Jack was cooking swordfish and salmon on the grill and had turned away to take a drink from his beer he had on the adjoining table. Before he knew it, one of the gulls Alek always fed, had swooped down and stole the large piece of swordfish right off the extremely hot grill.

After telling that story, everyone was paying closer attention to what Alek was doing. It was John who noticed the type of fish Alek was cleaning. He said, "Funny, I didn't think the stripers were running now."

CHAPTER 30

July 6 - Friday

Kevin and Erica had to be at work at eight, so Miranda and Jack tried to be as quiet as possible at five that morning so the kids could sleep a bit longer. With their bag filled with sunscreen, bug spray and bait, they walked the short distance over to the Franklin's. Liz and Richard were already there with the food for the outing. Liz had also stopped at Dunkin Donuts for a Box of Joe, coffee cups, sugar and creamers. She was a real lifesaver. No one had had time for their full caffeine fix.

John instructed the group as they boarded his boat on the location of the life jackets, head and where to stow their gear. Jack relayed that Alek hadn't left yet and that they may want to wait near the end of John's lagoon until Alek entered the channel to the Bay.

About ten to fifteen minutes later, they spotted Alek's boat making its way by them. He didn't seem to notice there was a boat just sitting there. John gave him plenty of lead, not wanting him to spot the group tailing him out to the Atlantic.

"I have always been very curious about his fishing spot" said Jack, "he is just so lucky. I don't think I have ever seen him come home empty handed."

They followed through to channel marker forty-nine and out to the Bay. It would take about twenty minutes to reach the inlet by Barnegat Light, passing Old Barney, the famous lighthouse. Miranda pulled out the dimenhydrinate tablets and popped one in her mouth with a swallow of coffee. She passed the box around to the rest of the group, asking if anyone needed some motion sickness medicine. The inlet and the ocean might be a bit choppy and she wanted to make sure she did not get sick on John's boat.

John speculated that Alek seemed to be headed to the Barnegat Light Reef which was a little over three miles from the inlet. The most popular spot being the Tires, an artificial reef made up of army tanks, small wrecks and concrete tires.

"I guess he is going for fluke today," said John. "There will be a number of other boats there so we won't stand out. We just have to be careful not to drift into him."

They settled into place and began to drift slowly. Jack brought out the live bait and began to put the small fish on the lines. Everyone took their fishing rods and cast into the ocean.

John made sure his boat was not too close to any other boat and joined the group at the stern.

He started, "I had a friend of mine from the Secret Service do a sweep of my house, car and boat. Nothing came up. Maybe it's because I have a good security system and outdoor cameras. I told him what happened to you and he promised to look into it. To date, there has been no report of this kind of activity here, but that doesn't mean there isn't a threat of some kind. There has been an increase in Russian activities and all the agencies are monitoring things closely."

"During conversations with the neighbors at the party, did anyone report anything suspicious or out of the ordinary? Liz, you seemed to have spent the entire time talking to Frederick. Did you get his life story?"

"Just about! So I started out by asking him where he was originally from and how he came to be in America. We knew he was foreign because he had an accent. He said he was born and raised in Austria, but when World War II broke out, he knew he would have to try to leave otherwise he might end up in a concentration camp or dead because he was Jewish. His family had been taken away and to this day, he had no idea what happened to them. He moved from family to family, working for his food and keep. He was able to remain somewhat hidden or invisible as he called it. With the war ending, he heard of networks by which Nazis or immigrants could escape to other countries. He had always been intrigued by South America. The Red Cross was able to get him papers and passage to Italy, where he had to work for months to earn enough to pay for his ticket on a ship to South America. Here he met an American who said he could help obtain transportation to Argentina and would finance his education at the university there. There would be conditions, of course, but if he studied hard and trained in a position of their choice, he would eventually be relocated to the United States where he could be granted citizenship."

"This seemed almost too good to be true, but Frederick had little choice and really wanted to study medicine and psychiatry. He did exceptionally well in school and his American friend was true to his word. I don't remember the exact year, but it was in the 1950s that he was moved to Philadelphia and set up his practice. Then in the 1960s, he bought a summer home here in Loveladies. He never said who his American benefactor was but it would have to be someone with clout and strings that could be pulled within our government."

"I know from readings Miranda and I have been doing about World War II and Nazis' escaping after the war, countries were using Nazis during the Cold War against the Soviets. The CIC/CIA was convinced the Nazis' networks would aid them in our fight of Communism. They were given new identities and put to work."

"John, Frederick's track from Austria to South America to the United States is the path some Nazi's took to escape after the war. Can you check him out to make sure he isn't an escaped war criminal?" asked Miranda. John agreed to an extensive background check.

"Liz, did you ask him anything that would lead you to believe he uses a computer or laptop?"

"No, but he did say he was old fashioned and used a Dictaphone to record his notes on patients. He even said he had to return next door to catch up on some work."

"Can you imagine what kind of information might be on that Dictaphone? He must have a service that does the transcription. What if his house is bugged? Is there any way to tell without letting him know we are looking?" Liz asked the group.

Miranda thought about whether she should divulge what she and Liz had been researching. She started, "Liz and I had real concerns over Chicky's death and his former employer. We started speculating all sorts of things. We really weren't certain where our ideas would lead so we went to the local library and started to research a few things."

She shared with the group the information they had gotten from Diane on Russian spies, the actual spies of Loveladies, Soviet submarines being off the coast, U.S. using ex-Nazi's to hunt communists and what kind of information Russian hackers were after. "I know I have joked about him being a Nazi, but is it possible he is who he says he is? There are just too many coincidences here. And finally, was Chicky's death an accident or something else? Did he know something or suspect something?"

"I will add that to my list of questions as this investigation continues. In the meantime, did anyone else notice that Alek left? I didn't see him reel in any fish and he appears to be heading further out to sea." John suggested the others pull in their poles and fired up the boat. "I am curious where he is going. His boat is much smaller than mine and it is a bit choppy out here. I am afraid we won't be able to follow him for long before he sees us."

The group agreed to continue to follow Alek into the Atlantic. John monitored their location on his GPS and how many miles that they were out to sea. He mentioned that international waters were about twenty-four miles out. At this point they were approximately eighteen miles from Barnegat Light. Miranda reminded the group that Russian subs had been spotted off the coast of New Jersey in international waters. After about forty-five minutes, they noticed Alek stopping. He dropped anchor, readied his poles, took a bucket and dumped what looks like chum into the water. John suggested that they do the same but tried to keep a reasonable distance so as not to frighten him with their closeness.

As the afternoon approached, Liz brought out the food and drink. A few fish had been caught, but no one had seen Alek catch anything. John went underneath to his galley and returned with a set of binoculars. He positioned himself so Alek wouldn't be able to see that he was being closely monitored.

Hours passed, and Alek had not caught one fish. In fact, he appeared to be playing with his phone or handheld GPS, John couldn't tell. He hadn't even checked to see if there was bait still on the hooks of the fishing poles he had dangling in the water. Jack suggested a couple of them jump in the water to make it look like they were having fun, not really paying any attention to Alek.

Three thirty in the afternoon, Alek pulled up his anchor and made ready to leave. John's boat was far enough from Alek's path home to not interfere with his passage. They followed him back as discreetly as possible.

Watching from a safe distance, they saw Alek make his way into the Barnegat Light inlet and veer left along the coastline, not back into the bay for Loveladies. Curious, John followed and they saw him dock his boat by Cassidy's Viking Village Fish Market. This store was located right on the docks by the fishing fleet, getting the freshest fish of the day.

Miranda suggested that John head back to their house so they could see Alek arrive home. A few minutes after 5 o'clock, Alek came down the lagoon and docked his boat. He unloaded his cooler and gear, washed off his boat and headed to his outdoor washing table. Opening his cooler, he took out a large red snapper. He held up the fish as his wife came out to greet him and he yelled, "Look what I caught today, isn't it a beauty?" Miranda and the rest of the group were amazed to find he was not this world class fisherman, but a fraud.

Keslie Patch-Bohrod

CHAPTER 31

July 6 - Friday

Everyone thanked John for the great day and for helping to catch some fish for dinner. He cleaned and filleted the fish and took them inside to the refrigerator. He told the group he was just going to run his boat home so he and Lori could have drinks with dinner. Even though he knew the lagoons well, he did not want to take any chances if he had too much to drink. He would walk back and join them in about twenty minutes.

Liz and Lori hurriedly pulled together a salad and a vegetable as the Jack and Richard fired up the grill for the fish. Miranda went out to her garden and collected thyme, parsley and basil. Adding some extra virgin olive oil and butter to a pan, she added chopped garlic and shallots.

After this had cooked for a few minutes she added the fresh herbs and a squeeze of lemon juice.

She would put some of the mixture on slices of toasted baguette and the rest would be brushed on the fish filets while they grilled.

The kids were still at work, the workers across the lagoon had quit early, so the adults would have a nice quiet dinner on the deck. Thankfully, there was a cool breeze coming off the bay and they decided to have dinner out on the deck and watch the sun set.

"There is nothing like freshly caught fish," said Jack.

"Alek's wife will never know the pleasure," said Richard, "if what we saw today is the norm."

"Things just get more and more curious." The group nodded at Miranda, but continued to watch Alek's house.

Miranda couldn't help but think there was more going on in Loveladies than met the eye. All they had been doing was speculating and feeding into their paranoia. Proof was needed and she wondered if John and his contacts would be able to 'sort the wheat from the chaff'.

CHAPTER 32

July 6 - Friday

What were they doing following me out to my fishing spots? My surveillance tapes don't indicate anything amiss. In fact, it appears they have no suspicions about their computers, phones or homes. Luckily, no one has discovered Frederick, Alek thought to himself

The information coming in is invaluable, from all economic sectors, especially pertaining to the Oyster Creek Nuclear Generating Station maintenance and systems. Won't New Jersey be surprised if there is a problem before it is shut down for good in October this year? Other power companies in the area have been taking over as they have geared down. With the hackers infiltrating these companies as well, there will be no power for quite a few people, and there might even be a bit radiation to add to the chaos. I really lucked out with that IT executive from Exelon. He had systems data that will allow us access to the facility and cooling pools. The other utilities have been planning for the decommission and have been picking up the slack. So far, there has been no additional news about the plant closing.

Alek pulled out the canister he had removed from the last fishing site today. It held a communique that outlined a number of posts he was to place on various social media accounts. Little warnings, nothing to incite panic right away. Just some more fake news or red herrings as they used to say. Lead them in one direction, while attacking them in the opposite direction. It would also provide a link that readers click for more information, which would just open the door for the hackers.

Maybe he would disobey his superiors and not post it. Why should the Americans be warned? Not knowing ahead of time would only lead to more chaos. He laughed to himself as he thought of what would happen. He had gotten access to so many companies and utilities and Russian hackers were working around the clock. Amtrak would not operate, there would be no electricity, no cable or satellite TV, no internet, transportation systems would not be able to operate, cell towers would be offline, no food or beverages would be delivered, and gas stations would not be able to pump gas. Of course, it would be important to render Fort Dix harmless, don't want the soldiers to be able to help out. Everything would be shut down on Labor Day Weekend, including Washington, D.C. Of course, there would be a trickle-down effect with transportation, food and gas as other regions would be affected. Everyone would be focusing on getting everything back up and running, all the while, Alek would be starting the process in other locations across the country. Before long, he would have the entire country in shambles and the leaders unable to lead. And then the fallout from what they had planned for Oyster Creek.

Each house was selected based on the owner's job and access to critical information that could be used to interrupt or terminate service. Fort Dix would even be compromised. Those planes flying over Loveladies now would not be able to land on Labor Day. Their systems and air traffic control would be shut down, and there would be no communications to commercial planes or aircraft carriers along the coast. Hackers were writing code faster than he could think. It would be impossible for even the very best technology experts to restore functioning to the hacked systems. It was brilliant how the hackers were able to get remote access to a company that provided power even if the power grid went out. A number of military forts throughout the U.S. were customers of theirs. One fort in particular in Maryland that would be affected defended against biological weapons. Nothing was safe. They had penetrated so deep.

Next on his to-do list was to find someone on the island that was high up on the food chain in law enforcement or government. If Homeland Security or the Pentagon could be hacked, that would be the icing on the cake.

Alek, this time, talking out loud to himself said, *'Joining the Loveladies Harbor Organization and the Loveladies Property Owners Association was a godsend. Almost everyone joins these organizations to learn about lagoon water conditions, property tax updates and to network with neighbors. For me, it provides a name and address on the lagoon or oceanfront. Starting with the lagoon homeowners, because of the easy access to their property, was key to getting this operation started. I ran background checks; identified employers or companies they worked for, through LinkedIn in many cases I got a resume and tasks performed. In some cases, I got two for one because people forgot to clear out old work data from their laptops and computers which gave me access to other companies. It is just so amazing how careless people are with their information.'*

He went out on his upper deck and watched the three couples work together to prepare their meal, remembering that he saw that third couple at the Craig's party. Alek thought to himself that he needed to find out who they were and what they did.

When the group was almost done with their dinner and evening, Alek left his house by car and drove over to the Craig's street. He parked a few houses down in one of the neighbor's driveway and waited.

The Goldbergs came out first, and walked down the street to return to their home. A few minutes later, the other couple came out and also walked down the street. Alek waited until they were at the end of the road and turned right on the boulevard before exiting his car and jogging after them. He saw them turn right at the next street and hurried to try and catch up. They entered the first house and he made a note of the number on the house.

After he retrieved his car, he returned home to his office where he accessed the Long Beach Township tax records. He entered the address and found the name of the owners of the house- John and Lori Franklin. A quick Google search told him all he needed to know about the couple, especially Mr. John Franklin.

Tomorrow, he would check out the house and surrounding area to see if he could gain access to the house. This was the man who might have the most valuable information of them all.

CHAPTER 33

July 7 - Saturday

It's going to be another humid, scorcher today, thought Miranda as she woke up. Jack was snoring lightly next to her. Realizing she would never get back to sleep because of the heat and the noise, she got up and let Maynard outside. She always enjoyed the quiet mornings in Loveladies. Usually, there was a breeze coming off the ocean this time of day. It was there, but it was very faint. They would need to keep the air conditioning on all day to be comfortable.

Miranda was relieved the party was over and all the guests had returned home. She just wanted life back to the normal, daily routine. There were still a few chores that had to be completed relating to the party. The keg, once completely emptied, had to be returned to Buy Rite Liquors off the island. The keg cozy, as she called it, which was the insulated surround, had to be returned to the party rental store. She hoped Kevin would take care of that before or after one of his shifts at work. The chafing dishes and stands would be taken to work by the kids and returned to Antonio.

Erica promised to wash all the sheets, blankets and pillowcases used by their friends that had stayed over. Miranda was certain that more than a drop or two of beer had been spilled on the bedding.

As she walked around the house toward the garden, Miranda couldn't help but feel uneasy. Her gut was telling her she needed to worry, about what she didn't know. Long Beach Island was no stranger to bad things. They had been broken into, as had others. There was even a murder one winter in Barnegat Light. Now, with Chicky possibly being murdered, it was too close to home.

She stepped over the two foot high fence that surrounded the garden. This had been put up to keep Maynard from getting into the garden and digging up the plants. Apparently, some of their Fourth of July guests could not find one of the many trash cans strategically placed around the backyard. Thankfully she had brought a garbage bag with her for the weeds, and began to pick up plates, cups and a wine bottle. She would sort out the recyclables later.

Jeez, what's with people? She thought. *Good thing these were behind the little fence where Maynard couldn't get to them. He is a good dog, but a dog nonetheless. He would have eaten whatever was left on the plate. Hell, he might have eaten the paper plate, and then gotten sick all over the place. He has no clue what is good for him. He just eats it.*

Miranda turned her attention back to her original chore. The weeds were really growing strong in the vegetable garden. They were almost taking over the herbs and tomato plants. As Miranda bent down to pull a few of the offending plants, Maynard started to whine near the fence that separated Frederick's property from theirs. Miranda went over to try and quiet Maynard down before he woke the neighborhood.

She remembered the sounds he was making; it reminded her of when she ran over a dead deer in the road near their home. She had parked the car in the garage and went to bed. The next morning, Maynard got up, began what she would label a panicked whine, and then began scratching the door to the laundry room, which led to the garage. She let him into the garage thinking maybe an intruder had gotten in. He immediately went under the car and tried to eat the pieces of dead, deer meat that had stuck to the undercarriage.

There was a putrid smell that hung in the hot, humid, morning air. She wondered if some of the guests had dumped some meat scraps where she couldn't see them. She couldn't imagine how a few meat scraps could smell like that, although it had been a few days since the party and it had been quite hot. The trash and recycling cans could get pretty ripe in a few days. She looked around through the weeds and under the plants, but found no food. No, she thought, it was much worse than that. She began to gag as the smell intensified and she rushed into the house to throw up.

Jack and the kids heard her retching in the bathroom and Jack rushed to her, "Honey, are you OK? What's the matter?"

Miranda couldn't talk, she could hardly breathe. She couldn't get the smell out of her nose; it seemed to permeate her skin and nose hairs. After about five minutes of heaving, she finally let out a yell, "Call the police! Call 911! Something is terribly wrong!"

Jack called 911 as he was walking outside to get the howling Maynard. As he approached the side of the house, the smell reached him and he immediately turned away. He knew exactly where it was coming from.

CHAPTER 34

July 7 - Saturday

As the police arrived, Jack was on the phone calling John to tell him he needed to come over right away. Miranda was out front talking with one of the officers as the other one was entering Frederick's house. Local emergency services arrived and awaited instructions. Do they rush a body to the hospital or quietly remove a body to the morgue?

The officer came out of the house with a rag over his mouth. He made a call on his police car radio and asked the onlookers to go back to their homes. John approached him with his credentials out and said, "My name is John Franklin and I work for a North New Jersey Sheriff's office. I may have some information that will be of interest to this investigation." The officer nodded and allowed John to accompany him into the house.

More law enforcement vehicles pulled down the road; the medical examiner from Toms River arrived and technicians began their collection of samples.

John came out of the house and went over to the Craig's. "Please go inside and wait until the scene is cleared and Frederick is removed. I will get in touch with you and we will schedule to meet somewhere. In the meantime, please take note of everyone you see, what they do and where they go, if you can. We have officers around and they will observe, but you have better local knowledge than they do. You can tell if something or someone is off."

Miranda, Jack and the kids went back into the house. Maynard had finally quieted down but was still alert and attentive to all that was going on around the house. He let out a random bark as the ambulance left with Frederick's body. Miranda staked her place by the front door and watched the activity. Maynard did the same at the sliding glass doors to the backyard, watching his 'doggy TV'.

An officer approached the Craig's front door and Miranda let him into the house. He introduced himself as Officer Stevens and asked if he could take a statement about what she discovered and get some background about the neighbor. Miranda brought cups of coffee, creamer, and sugar to the table as they sat down.

"Mrs. Craig, could you please start at the beginning and tell me what happened? If the medical examiner feels anything is amiss, there will be detectives coming back to question you in more detail."

"Frederick had come to our Fourth of July party on Wednesday. He seemed just fine. As a matter of fact, he spent most of the time talking with our neighbor, Liz Goldberg, who lives across the lagoon from us. She can tell you more about their conversation and if he told her if he was sick or had any health issues. They spoke for over an hour and a half. I know he had a plate of food and maybe a beer or two. He came to see Jack and me before he left, thanking us for our hospitality and that he had some work he had to complete. This morning, I was outside with our dog and had started to do some weeding in the garden when Maynard became quite agitated. Then, I smelled something horrible. I just knew something was wrong and I had Jack call 911. That is all I know. As I said, you need to talk with Liz."

Liz and Richard saw the commotion from across the lagoon. They knew better than to get in the way, but Liz was beside herself. She had spent the better part of an afternoon talking with Frederick and now he was dead. She needed to talk with Miranda; they needed to talk with John.

As they were standing on their dock, they noticed that all the neighbors were also out. Except Alek and he was not out fishing.

CHAPTER 35

July 8 - Sunday

"We bought this house for quiet!" Miranda yelled at Jack. "This is supposed to be the quiet town, the place where nothing happens! It has been noisy and horrible all summer long! I can't stand it! The Haverford's have been constructing all hours of the day. Alek wakes us up before the sun comes up. Now this! A second death on this lagoon!"

"Miranda, you really need to get a grip. There is nothing you can do. You just have to calm down and deal with it."

"You don't have to deal with it, you just leave! The kids go to work. I am stuck here taking care of the house, making meals, grocery shopping and making things nice for all of you. I am stuck here day in and day out! The minute I don't do what I am supposed to do, you will lose it. It reminds me of that picture I saw on Facebook. There is a kitchen; the mother is sitting on chair with a kid in her lap, kids all around, a dog and a big mess. Her hair is knotted. Food remains on the counter. The husband walks in. She says, "You wonder what I do all day? Well, today I didn't do it. Is that how you want me to deal with it? I have been trying to hold it together but this has just pushed me over the edge!"

Jack picked up the phone and called Liz. "Liz, I need you to take Miranda to the movies or for lunch or drinks or something. Get her out of the house for the rest of the day. For however long it takes. Go to Atlantic City, I don't care. Distract her. Richard and I will fend for ourselves."

Liz picked up Miranda and suggested they drive to the other end of the island for lunch. "Let's go the Gables and do high tea! We haven't done that in a long time. Remember how quaint that is?"

It took them forty-five minutes to get to the other end of the island to the Gables. Traffic was horrific this time of year. Not only were there renters and beach goers clogging the road from one end of the island to the other, all the traffic lights were operational (off season they blinked yellow) and the speed limit was only twenty-five to thirty-five miles per hour.

Liz used her Bluetooth connection to call ahead and made a reservation for two for high tea. The Gables was a beautiful Old Lady, a Victorian home restored to its old time glory. Purples and pinks, lace tablecloths, flowers everywhere. They were seated at their table overlooking the ocean. Liz took charge and ordered Lady Grey tea and the standard high tea service of finger sandwiches, scones and delicate pastries. The Gables also had a liquor license, so she ordered a bottle of Sancerre to accompany their meal. She requested the wine be served first and right away.

Once their first glass was poured, Miranda couldn't contain herself any longer. "I can't thank you enough for getting me out of there. Jack knows me too well. I was ready to kill someone, anyone. You can't imagine the smell Liz. It is still in my nose. I don't know if I will ever be able to go out in my garden again without thinking how badly it smelled. Thankfully, I didn't go into his house. I don't know how the police or John can deal with that. Did you tell John everything you discussed with Frederick? I think there must be something of value from your conversation that will help the investigation."

Liz replied that she had told the police everything she could remember. They would just have to wait and let the authorities do their job. If there was a connection, they would find it and deal with it.

The tea service arrived and Miranda decided she must make the best of things and move on. She took several long, deep breaths to calm her. They enjoyed the cucumber and butter, watercress, and smoked salmon sandwiches on the lower tier. Next came the cranberry and orange scones with clotted cream. Finally, the top tier was filled with pastries and fresh strawberries, blackberries and figs to finish off the feast.

"I am pitiful. All it takes is some good food, a little bit of wine and I forget about someone dying," confessed Miranda.

"You just needed a break from your morbid thoughts, Miranda. I know you care. We can't do anything to help until we can compartmentalize and be objective. That may sound cold, well so be it. He had no one to look out for him, so maybe we need to take over that role."

"I don't know why I am having such a problem with this" admitted Miranda. "I didn't really know him or care about him. He was just a neighbor that we would see a few times during the summer and not even socially except for our party. I would have thought you would be in shambles over this being that you had spent so much time with him at our party. I think you really started to like him!"

Liz replied, "It's probably because I didn't smell him."

Jack asked John later that night, "Do you think Miranda and the kids are safe? This is the second death here on the lagoon in one year. I am a bit worried."

"Jack, both deaths right now seem accidental and/or natural. Let's not get worried until we have to. I will get the locals to keep a lookout on this end of the island more often. They requested video footage from the neighbors with cameras on your street, so we will see if anyone was around that might have seen something or done something they shouldn't have."

CHAPTER 36

July 9 - Monday

Everyone was back at work except for Miranda and Liz. There was yellow crime scene tape all around Frederick's property. John had told Jack that police officers would be in contact with them today and that they would need to give statements. There was definitely something suspicious about Frederick's death.

Detectives arrived at Miranda's at eight that morning, introducing themselves as Detectives Travers and Williams. Miranda opened the door and suggested they sit in the living room. They asked her to recount the events of the previous day and whether she knew if Frederick Wasserman had any health issues or enemies. She provided what information she could, repeating what she had told the other officer the day before, noting that he was a very quiet neighbor and appeared to be well liked.

Before the officers left, Miranda decided to ask them about Chicky. She had never been questioned about his death and thought that odd. Even though she and her family had left that same morning, she thought a thorough investigation would have included conversations with all the neighbors, whether they were present at the time or not.

"Do you think this has anything to do with Chicky Haverford's death?"

"Mrs. Craig, why would you ask that?" Officer Travers said.

"Don't you think it strange that two deaths occur on the same lagoon in less than one year?"

"Mr. Haverford accidentally drowned last year and it appears that Mr. Wasserman died of unknown causes a few days ago. I don't know why you would think they were related. We won't know anything more about Dr. Wasserman's death until the autopsy is complete. In addition, both men were elderly. Is there something you know that you should tell us?"

Miranda thought for a minute then decided that the officer needed to be aware of what was going on. "Please speak with John Franklin, I believe he left his name and number with the other officer yesterday. Also, please speak with my neighbor, Liz Goldberg and have her tell you about the conversation she had with the deceased at our party on the fourth of July. I know she is home, so why don't I take you over there and she can tell you what she knows."

The detectives allowed Miranda to accompany them to the Goldberg's home, more out of expediency than procedure. Officer Stevens had informed them of John Franklin's involvement and his background, which made them very curious.

Miranda texted Liz that she and two policemen were on their way over to interview her. Liz opened the front door to greet them as they pulled onto her property. Introductions were made after everyone was inside and they settled on the couches in the spacious living room.

Detective Williams started, "Mrs. Goldberg, we understand you had a lengthy conversation with Dr. Wasserman on July fourth at the Craig's party. Would you mind telling us, in as much detail as possible, about what you discussed?"

"I saw Frederick walk over to the Craig's about noon. I spoke to Miranda about what she thought he would like to drink and she suggested a glass of the Blue Moon draft they had in the keg and to include a slice of orange. He had had that last year at their party and had enjoyed it. I greeted him, handed him the beer and suggested we sit down and get better acquainted. We have talked before but never in much detail. This year, Miranda, Jack, Richard and I were intent on learning as much as possible about our neighbors, trying to become friendlier. Everyone is always in such a hurry or has company, and we never really get a chance to socialize. The Craig's party is the only time when most of the neighbors come together in one place."

"He told me he was originally from Austria. Near the end of World War II he was able to get papers and passage to Italy. From there, he went to South America where he settled in Buenos Aires. He was accepted at Universidad de Buenos Aires where he studied psychiatry. And it was Chicky Haverford that helped him enter the United States and set up practice in Philadelphia. This was in the early 1950s. He didn't go into any details as to how they met or how Chicky ended up helping him. And get this; Chicky was the one that suggested he buy a summer home in Loveladies and he moved here in the late 1950s or early 1960s. His patients are the wealthy businessmen and women of Philadelphia and Washington, D.C. Those that live around the Capital don't want it known that they see a psychiatrist. So they take the two hour train from D.C. to Philadelphia for their visits. Apparently, he is very well respected."

Miranda had been quiet up until this point. "After I learned that Chicky Haverford had died in that strange way, I looked up his obituary. It stated that he had worked for the CIA in Langley, Virginia. Don't you think it is too much of a coincidence that you had an individual with a very unique background as Frederick did, and a neighbor, Chicky, that happened to work for the CIA who is also dead, and they both had homes in Loveladies which were built by two known ex-Soviet spies?"

Both detectives had been taking copious notes throughout the interview. Detective Travers stopped and asked, "Did Dr. Wasserman say anything else about how he got to the United States, how he started his practice or what he really did in exchange for his livelihood?"

"No," Liz said. "We talked for quite a while and had a few beers and some food. Miranda had ordered this really good seafood pasta for the party and he was very taken with it. I think he had two helpings. I could tell at that point he was beginning to tire and he said he really had to get back to his house. He had brought work home because he was very behind in his dictation of patient notes. He said his goodbye, and went to find Miranda and Jack to thank them. This was around four or four thirty. That was the last time I saw him."

"Are you sure he said he had work to do?" asked Detective Williams.

"Yes, I believe he said he had a stack of files he had to work through before Friday when he would return to Philadelphia. He had a patient he was seeing in his office then."

"If that is true, then I think we have a problem, because there were no files in his house or car, and no Dictaphone or recording device."

CHAPTER 37

July 9 - Monday

Alek sat in his special room with the door locked. Each of the five flat screen computer monitors was on so he could follow what was happening. He heard the interviews in the Craig and Goldberg homes. Since he had removed all the listening devices from the house, he had to look through the window to see the police coming and going through Frederick's home and effects. The other two screens showed computer activity on the various laptops under surveillance, shifting from one location to another.

There was no way the police could connect him to either of the two deaths. It had been over a year since Chicky's and the police had not come back with any more questions. He knew eventually, they would be around to ask him what he knew about Frederick but he would plead ignorance, saying only they were casual friends that would go to dinner once in a while. His wife hadn't seen him leave on July fourth when he went to visit Frederick that night, and she assumed he was locked away in his office all night doing work.

He really should start to think about a contingency plan should the authorities find a reason to search his property. He had a small storage area under the floorboards where he could secure his pertinent data, surveillance equipment and his 'chemicals'. Maybe now would be a good time to put a few things away; he really didn't need all this stuff out in the room. The computer monitors could easily be justified. Working for a think tank, he would have to be up to date on the latest news from CNN, Fox, MSNBC, while doing research on the internet.

He knew that Frederick's death would eventually be attributed to the shellfish poisoning and he had hoped it would be linked to tainted food the Craig's served. Thankfully, he had overheard a conversation between the Craig woman and his neighbor discussing who the caterer was and what they planned on serving. After researching best poisons, he determined the Saxitoxin would be the best and most logical fit.

155

The fact that they knew about the files and that they were missing hadn't been anticipated. Once they found out Frederick was deliberately poisoned, they might speculate his assailant took the files to cover his tracks, although he couldn't be sure he found them all. Frederick came to the shore each weekend so it is possible he brought more work here than Alek knew. Still, the lack of files could be good. The police might think it was one of his patients that killed him or a fellow CIA operative to cover his government involvement. One thing for certain, he would have to get into Frederick's Philadelphia home and office immediately and remove any evidence of his surveillance and search for the rest of his files.

CHAPTER 38

July 9 - Monday

Jack sat in his office with a cup of coffee staring at his computer monitors. He was tuned in to the different financial news networks watching the various markets going up and down. Today, though, he was more worried about his wife and kids than the market fluctuations.

He and Miranda had been married over twenty years and he had never seen her this upset. She was such a strong and determined woman, that's what he loved most about her.

It was more of the determined side that worried him right now. He knew she was digging into this, getting herself smack dab in the middle of things and bringing Liz along with her. She used to be able to take of herself but that was a long time ago before the kids were born.

This situation was also quite a bit different from Workers Compensation fraud. This was possible espionage and probable murder. Two types of crime she wasn't equipped to deal with.

His business was going great and his client list kept growing. She never minded the hours he put in, he loved what he did and the people he worked with. Miranda always seemed busy and happy especially during the summer when she could relax at the shore and allow the ennui to set in.

But now it was different. She was frazzled, distant and almost paranoid. Maybe she needed to talk with someone. She always saw the dark side of life, and imagined the worst. Guess that had to do with her previous work.

Now she was dealing with this current business of Frederick's body being discovered next door. How did she even know that's what death smelled like?

John had said it was a gruesome scene. He had been dead awhile and with the heat the flies and maggots were busy feeding on his body. Good thing Miranda hadn't decided to go check up on him. What would have happened if she had seen him in that state of decomposition?

CHAPTER 39

July 10 - Tuesday

It was going to be a beautiful day. Miranda turned on The Weather Channel to see the details. It would only get up to about seventy-seven degrees, a wonderful breeze, with relatively low humidity. It would be a perfect day to try to bake her Aunt Joyce's egg bread. She had tried at home, but it was always too cold in the house and the bread didn't rise as it should. Her Aunt's bread was always buttery yellow and would rise well above the bread pan when baked.

The kids were still asleep; she remembered them telling her they would not have to go into work until ten that morning. Letting them sleep, she leashed up Maynard for an early morning walk in the cool, crisp air. He felt it too; there was a definite change in the air from the previous days of hot and humid mugginess.

Maynard usually had his route down their street, turn left at the boulevard then walk a couple of streets and decide it was too hot and want to turn back. Today, he pulled slightly on the leash and Miranda knew they would enjoy a much longer walk.

When they left their property, he insisted on sniffing around Frederick's yard. This had never happened before and Miranda thought she should let him. As Jack always said, "Trust your dog, they do things for a reason."

Obviously, he still smelled death and the many people who had come and gone from the investigation. After about five minutes, he sniffed his way to the end of the property by the dock and stopped. She had to physically pull him back to the road and onto the boulevard.

When they got to the next street, Liz and Richard's, he wanted to go down that way. Strange, thought Miranda, he never wanted to go down the side streets. They made it as far as Alek's house and Maynard became agitated, smelling all around the front of the property. Miranda had to forcefully pull him away again and continue on for the rest of their walk.

Finally, back on the boulevard, they walked past the Loveladies Tennis Club where there were lessons and matches going on. Kids and older couples really enjoyed the club. Maynard stopped to graze on some grass and watch the tennis balls volley back and forth. Tugging at his leash, they walked as far as the Long Beach Island Foundation of the Arts and Sciences. The parking lot was full of cars and Miranda could see parents taking their children in for some of the summer camp activities. Members also enjoyed the pottery and painting classes. Miranda at one time had even taken a creative writing class there. They have so many wonderful things for the community to partake in. Sensing that he had had enough, Miranda crossed the street and returned back home. She would have to tell Jack, the Goldberg's and John about what Maynard did and see what they thought.

Walking into the house, Miranda saw that the kids had been up, made breakfast and left, leaving her with the mess to take care of. She got busy emptying the dishwasher and putting the dirty dishes in the slots. She thought to herself how her life had changed since having kids and not working full time. This brought a silent laugh; not working full time! Who was she kidding? She still worked full time but no one really considers what housewives do as 'real work' and there definitely was no paycheck.

She had had a chance to read a bit more in her novel, and promised herself that she would run to the store while the bread dough was rising and buy the ingredients for her dinner. Surf City had a farmers' market on Tuesday outside of the firehouse where she could find freshly picked vegetables. The frittata described in her book sounded like a good idea and the kids could eat the leftovers for their breakfast tomorrow with slices of toasted homemade bread.

After the kitchen was clean, Miranda took a look at the recipe card for the bread. Most she understood, but when she came to 'scald two cups of milk', she was baffled. Bringing the laptop out to the kitchen island, she looked up how to scald milk.

Making bread was no easy matter and after she set the kneaded mess into an oiled, covered bowl, her shoulders and hands ached terribly. She guessed that was why peasant women were so strong.

It would be an hour or so for the bread to rise for the first time, so she fed Maynard, grabbed her purse and ran to Country Corner Market for her lunch items and the farmers' market for her dinner ingredients. Today's sandwich would be pastrami and potato salad. She might even be able to sit outside by the pool and read a bit more of her book if the construction noise wasn't too loud.

But when she got back and had her sandwich made, the Goldberg's and another neighbor were having their weekly landscaping work done. The hedge trimmers and leaf blowers were making as much noise as the construction workers. Miranda was becoming distraught. She was going to have no peace and quiet this entire summer.

She looked around at the other properties on their lagoon and thought of the ones on their street. There were at least seven or eight that she could think of as possible 'tear downs', meaning that if someone bought them, they would tear them down and build a big monstrosity like the Haverford's and she would never have another quiet summer at the shore. Between the undetected break-ins, buggings and the relentless noise, she began to wonder if it would be better the sell the house. This wasn't the Loveladies she knew and loved.

All the joy of baking bread seemed to be sucked out of her. She reluctantly returned to the chore and finished the remaining tasks, putting two loaves into the oven to bake.

Keslie Patch-Bohrod

CHAPTER 40

July 11 - Wednesday

It was like living in a fishbowl. No, it was like the Hitchcock movie *Rear Window* with Jimmy Stewart and Grace Kelly. Jimmy was wheelchair bound with a broken leg. He didn't have a TV on to watch, so he spent his day looking out of his window at the courtyard and the windows of the other apartments. He watched and kept track of the other tenants and eventually suspected a murder was committed in an apartment across the way.

Miranda sat at the outdoor bar on their deck drinking her morning coffee before the construction workers began their day at seven thirty. She watched carefully to see if anyone was in the house yet. The town had regulations as to the hours that builders and landscapers (those that make noise) could work. Miranda had begun to keep regular tabs on them and called when they broke the rules. She had had enough of it. The Haverfords weren't the only people who lived here.

She looked across the lagoon and could see in Liz's house and saw that she, too, was up and having breakfast. Over at Alek's, his wife was out in her garden tending the vegetables and deadheading her flowers. There was no sign of Alek or his boat, so she assumed he was out early again fishing.

The Germans, next to Alek, seemed to have a bunch of family members joining them for the week. They had been enjoying the sun, jet skiing and boating, also contributing to the noise on the lagoon.

Do these neighbors pay as much attention to the Craig's as she did of them? Miranda wondered do they sit and watch her now as she drinks her coffee or were they oblivious to the goings on around them. Was that how an intruder was able to take advantage? People weren't observant, which allowed him/her to break in and watch their lives from the inside rather than like Miranda who watched from the outside?

The kids got up and found Miranda outside. The two were dressed in shorts, T-shirts and running shoes and told her they were going out for run before breakfast and work at eleven thirty. They were trying to work off the deli food they had been nibbling on for over a month.

CHAPTER 41

July 11

As his usual habit, Alek left in his boat about six in the morning. He wasn't going out on the water today; he had other business to attend to. He drove his boat to a nearby marina, docked and sought out one of the mechanics telling him he suspected some engine trouble. He asked if someone would be able to take a look at it today, he would return later and pick it up. He walked outside and made a cell phone call to the Enterprise Car Rental company in Manahawkin and asked to be picked up because he needed to rent a car.

He would drive into Philadelphia and visit Frederick's home and office there, removing any evidence of his surveillance. He would also have to search to see if Frederick had any evidence as to what he, Alek, was up to. He probably did not have much and that was why he was trying to get a taped, detailed confession the other night. Luckily he was able to nip that in bud.

Alek knew from his surveillance Frederick and Chicky were working together over the years to uncover Soviet spying activities as well as domestic sabotage. Chicky had targeted a number of individuals for Frederick to subtly question under the guise of therapy. Other individuals were investigated by other means. They had been quite successful in terminating a number of attempts to disrupt the government.

By monitoring their response and actions, Alek and his co-conspirators were able to develop plans that defied detection. They did not speak on the phone, write emails, or talk in person. They went back to basics where they could, and other times passed coded messages and encrypted flash drives. They communicated only through the open water drop site in the Atlantic Ocean. He would go out on his boat almost daily. He would drop a canister of information somewhere in the ocean or pick one up .They passed information in a water tight canister with special GPS tracking so that it could be found at any time. His GPS transponder would alert him if, when and where there was a response to be picked up. The canister had to be opened a certain way or acid was released and all the materials inside were destroyed. They never dropped messages at the same location or the same time. It was done during the normal process of fishing. One time, Alek had to dissect a fish that had eaten one of the smaller canisters.

The Coast Guard was always a problem and kept them on their toes. Occasionally, they would request to board his boat as part of a routine safety check. They watched everyone, always looking for evidence that a crime was being committed. Of course, there were no drugs or contraband items on Alek's boat. They weren't looking for paper or what he was carrying. Even so, he was always able to burn it or open the canister and release the acid before they could board and inspect his vessel. With the number of boats in the bay, inlet and Atlantic Ocean, it wasn't often that he was stopped. He always tried to navigate safely and obey the maritime laws- except those that pertained to him passing on secrets to take down the Capitalist pigs.

Alek, like Nathan Silvermaster, was born in Russia. He had come with his parents to the United States when he was young. His father was an Ambassador of the Soviet Union to the United States. Alek was a young boy at the time and was very impressionable. His father demanded he remain loyal to Mother Russia even though he was living in America. He was introduced to Silvermaster and Ullmann when he was in his late twenties, and began his grooming for his present day role.

Alek was able to get in and out of Frederick's house and office within two hours. It appeared that the police had not been there yet. Possibly, they didn't believe there was any foul play in his death or they just weren't able to coordinate it. Either way, Alek felt like luck was on his side.

There wasn't much in either location. Alek was a bit stunned by the minimal surroundings. Both places had very little furniture or personal items. He thought Frederick must have been a very lonely man. He couldn't find where the patient records were kept. He knew the notes were dictated and typed with copies going to Chicky. But where were Frederick's copies? He had looked through his financial statements looking for other properties or safe deposit boxes, but found nothing of value. He had no computers or secretary, no family or children. Where did he store his records? He removed all listening devices.

Alek was pulling onto the street from the underground parking lot of Frederick's office, when he saw several police cars and unmarked vehicles park in front of the building. He couldn't believe his good timing.

CHAPTER 42

July 12 - Thursday

John Franklin, luckily, was still in good standing with the Secret Service and was able to pull a few strings with his former boss, Ray Milford. He was granted access to the confidential information that had been put together concerning Chicky Haverford (whose real name was Warner Haverford), and Dr. Frederick Wasserman. John had spoken with Ray after Jack's visit concerning the spyware and bugs placed in their homes. He had been aware of various agencies currently investigating an increase of Soviet activity in the area. There were multiple potential targets and all agencies were on full alert not only for Soviets but other domestic and international terrorists.

Each man had a dossier comprised of memos, reports, detailed transcribed conversations and tapes concerning Soviet activities and individuals in Pennsylvania, New Jersey, Delaware, New York, Virginia and Washington, D.C. It included names and addresses, suspected planned events and potential impacts on various aspects of the United States economy. The government had been aware for a long time that the battleground was changing from man to man combat to cyber warfare.

In reviewing the names listed, none looked familiar to John and none were listed in the Long Beach Island tax records or membership directories of the Harbor Organization or the Property Owners Association. Was there a connection between what Frederick and Chicky were working on and the new crimes? He would have to speak with Homeland Security and especially the Secret Service, which did more than just protected the President and elected officials. It investigated financial and electronic crimes, terrorism and drug trafficking to name a few of its missions.

He would have to get the local police, Homeland Security, and the Secret Service together to go over what had been learned and how it might be impacting the overall investigation.

CHAPTER 43

July 13 - Friday

Kevin and Erica had come home from work and went out for another run. After dinner, they informed Miranda they were going out with their friends. Miranda would be by herself again and it happened to be Friday the thirteenth; Jack would be coming down as usual on Saturday. After she cleaned up the dinner dishes and the stove, Miranda took Maynard outside to do his business. It was already dark out and only a few of the houses had any outdoor lights on. She had to be careful where she walked because she hadn't cleaned up after Maynard's early morning business.

Maynard, as was his custom, began by sniffing around the outdoor table and bar area hoping for some remnant of food left behind. Then he would move to the outdoor couches and over to the garden area. All of a sudden he began to bark incessantly, jumping at the fence by the shed. He appeared to be barking at something over the fence in Frederick's yard. It was not his usual bark; it was more of a warning bark. After his tracking behavior the other day, Miranda was a bit worried.

Miranda called, "Maynard, come!" Nothing, he kept barking. "Maynard, come!" He seemed to bark even more. He was trying to shove his head between the slats in the fence. She needed to get him away from the fence before he hurt himself or got hurt from whoever was over there. She also didn't want to get too close to the fence for fear of what might be lurking.

The only thing Miranda could do was to run inside and grab her phone so she could use the flashlight function and call 911, if needed. The kids, having not left yet, followed her out, shouting "What's the matter now?"

Flashlight on, Miranda approached the fence cautiously, thinking an intruder might be hiding on the other side, maybe even the killer returning to the scene of the crime. The police tape was still up around the property and the police continued to patrol the street a bit more frequently than in the past. It would be easy for them to miss someone scrunching themselves up in the bushes.

The light caught something and she saw movement around one of the bushes by the fence line right where Maynard was going crazy. She inched forward, the kids behind her. Something shiny flashed at them and Erica squealed, startling Miranda and Kevin. They both jumped back and bumped into Erica. Miranda moved forward again aiming the light at the top of the fence and into Frederick's backyard trying to see if anyone was there. They heard rustling in between Maynard's barking, and then they finally saw them; white shiny orbs at the top of the bush.

Kevin ran up and grabbed Maynard by the collar and tried to pull him away. They all spotted the prowler and he even had a mask on his face as he was sitting atop Frederick's grape bush.

Raccoon. Not too many of those down here. Occasionally, one would be spotted around a trash can or dead on the side of the road. This one had a taste for the grape.

Relieved it was nothing to be concerned about, other than keeping the dog away, the four of them returned to the inside. Miranda would have to make sure there were no food scraps left outside, and the trash cans had their lids on securely. She would also have to keep closer tabs on Maynard because she didn't want him getting into any scrapes with a raccoon that could possibly be rabid. She might have to go and pick the grapes from that bush to keep the raccoon away.

Miranda was quite unsettled by the raccoon. Sure it was just an animal wandering around the neighborhood, but had it not been for Maynard, she wouldn't have known about it. It could have been a person. Someone could have been sneaking around Frederick's property or using Frederick's property to spy on her. Someone could easily walk onto their property from Frederick's bulkhead over to their dock and up onto their backyard. She had proved it possible to gain access to someone's house by use of the lagoon when she entered the Goldberg's house. She would have to be even more vigilant.

Having a dog as protective as Maynard provided some degree of comfort. With the kids out late at night and the two deaths on the lagoon, she was grateful for her noisy watchdog tonight on this Friday the thirteenth and the fact that she could turn on all the outdoor lights. Every last one of them.

CHAPTER 44

July 13 - Friday

Alek was dozing in his favorite rocking chair on his upper deck. He woke with a start at the dog barking like a mad man. He watched as his neighbors and the dog stared at something in Frederick's bushes. Hearing them say raccoon, he got an idea to eliminate the dog. People sometimes put out strychnine to get rid of rodents and other scavengers. Maybe that would be a bit too obvious. He would do a bit of research and find something that would take care of that dog, maybe not permanently but for a few days.

CHAPTER 45

July 14 - Saturday

Miranda's anger had been simmering on the back burner ever since they found out their house and electronics had been bugged. For the sake of not alerting whoever it was, they had been tiptoeing around, barely speaking and being extremely careful as to the content of any conversation. She did not know how much longer she could take it. The only thing making it somewhat easy was the fact the kids were working long hours and Jack was up North in his office five to six days out of the week, so she really didn't have anyone to talk to during the day expect maybe Liz or the dog.

Liz, too, was finding it extremely difficult. They decided to create a simple code. If either one of them had information or just needed to vent about the situation, they would call and use the code. Miranda would talk about her garden, since this wasn't something she would normally talk to Liz about. Liz would talk about window treatment options for her house. Then they would rendezvous on the boulevard.

Everyone was anxiously awaiting news from John when the devices could be removed from their homes, laptops and phones. But so far, Homeland, FBI and local law enforcement agencies hadn't uncovered a trace of evidence. If they removed them too early, it might trigger some event and the hackers would disappear. If they waited too long, the hackers would accomplish their goal whatever that was and they still might not find them.

In addition, John had told them it wasn't prudent to have a bunch of feds running around the island. Number one, they would stand out like a sore thumb and two, they might scare the guy into hiding, assuming it is only one person. They didn't want him to hide or slow down. They wanted to catch and stop him from whatever he was doing.

They only had a few people working on this since there was no concrete evidence. There was malware all over the place, not just here. What made this most interesting was that it was physically loaded with no real evidence of a break in. Just the telltale signs of listening devices and computer tampering. A few knickknacks moved about and that was it. No broken locks or windows. No fingerprints. It was a real conundrum.

Miranda's skin began to crawl as she saw Alek walk from his house to his boat. She thought it odd and creepy the way he surveyed his domain and each and every house surrounding his on the lagoon. Her Gladys meter was ticking loudly like a Geiger counter coming in contact with a large amount of radioactive material. Alek's movements reminded her of countless Workers' Compensation claimants who had something to hide and watched for any sign of detection.

CHAPTER 46

July 14 - Saturday

Alek looked around the lagoon at the old houses he helped to build. Not only was he proud of the workmanship of the ones left standing after all these years, he was also proud of the fact that he could get into any one of them at a moment's notice. He knew the ins and outs of all the windows, doors and sliders. Plus, he was a locksmith, self-trained and had made keys for most of the houses over the years during the winter when no one was about. The people who left keys in the shower made his job easier. All he had to do was make an impression of their key and put it right back.

When the new houses, like the Haverford's, were being built, he went through them during the construction process at night and found what he needed to know to get in undetected.

A lot of people wondered around new construction on the island. It was a past time for many folks, to look at the big houses being built. Most of the builders didn't mind, in fact they liked it. It gave them a chance to promote themselves; you never knew when someone would be in the market and want you to build them a big house too. What they didn't like were the looky loos that would come through, then come back on the weekend when no one was around and steal wood, nails, siding or tile. Alek didn't like them either, because they might catch him doing something and remember his face.

CHAPTER 47

July 16 - Monday

Miranda received a call from the Surf City Library on Monday morning at nine.

Diane said, "I just got that book you ordered the other day and wondered if you would be able to come in and get it this morning? Maybe you want to bring Liz with you? She might be interested in the new magazines that had come in. The best time for me would be ten o'clock; does that sound good to you?" Miranda agreed.

Hanging up the phone she thought, '*What the heck was that all about?*' She immediately called Liz and told her about her tomatoes. She asked Liz if she wanted to run out to Home Depot with her. She needed something to keep the bugs and snails out of her garden. She would pick her up at nine thirty. Liz said she would love to.

Miranda picked up Liz and they began to drive. Liz said, "Ok, what's up?"

"I just got the strangest call from Diane at the library telling me my book came in and there were magazines for you. I think something is up because I certainly didn't order a book from the library and I don't think you are interested in magazines, are you? I don't know what it is, but I am sure we will find out soon enough."

They pulled into the library parking lot and entered the building. Diane spotted them right away and motioned for them to join her in one of the conference rooms. They spotted John Franklin with a few other individuals in the room. John introduced them to the other people; some were from the FBI, Homeland Security, Secret Service, NSA and local law enforcement.

"Ladies, sorry for the cloak and dagger, but I just wanted to keep you up to date with what is happening. We have been meeting with a number of different agencies, some of them here today. As I told you a few days ago, we still have no credible evidence or information as to what is going on. What we do know is that *something* is going on here. We have come up with a plan to try and figure out who is involved and what they are trying to achieve.

Basically, background checks will be run on everyone owning property in Loveladies first, and then branching out as necessary. We will be looking for anything that stands out. In addition to that, we have been working with Atlantic City Electric, Comcast, Verizon and other internet providers on the island. They have agreed to a massive shut down of services for a period of time. This will allow us to send in agents, instead of company technicians, to take a look at all the devices to get a handle on this problem. We need to see if this is island wide or smaller in scope."

"If malware is found, it will be removed and the residents will be told that a power surge destroyed their hard drive. Their employer will be contacted and we will work with them to create "new" information to replace what was on the computer. The Loveladies Harbor Organization and the Loveladies Property Owners Association will be given letters to include in an email blast to all members about the problem- that a power surge may have damaged some computers and the various internet providers will be sending out technicians to help resolve the issue and make repairs to their systems. Hopefully, the homeowners will get this email on their phone or device at the primary residence. This will allow us to identify residents that most likely would have access to confidential and/or critical information. Homeland Security and the Secret Service can work with these facilities and companies' top Information Technology Offices to devise a plan to install fictitious information that would require hackers to re-do whatever they started with the bogus information, thereby neutralizing the effects. It would also give the companies time to fix and protect their systems against potential future attacks."

"We will do spot checks in Barnegat Light and Harvey Cedars just to make sure there are no breaches there. If we need to, we will expand out as necessary. We will try to question residents about their use of tradesmen- who, what, where, when and why. We can run background checks on the workmen or at least have a timeline when a key was in the shower or outside or how they got access to perform the work."

"We are also checking with all residents that have outside video equipment. I know local law enforcement has been lucky catching people on video stealing building supplies from construction sites. We hope we will find footage of someone breaking into a home."

"We are checking out the manufacturers of the devices that have been planted and trying to trace them. We will plot all this out and see if there are any connections. What we know so far, is that the devices in your house and Liz's have come from the same manufacturer. Once we have a bigger list of those involved we can begin to look for patterns. But until then, I need you to continue with the silent treatment and keep your eyes open. "

"The power surge will happen very soon, and then you will be able to get back to normal."

"Whoever is doing this will either know we are on to them or just thinks this is some very bad luck that will severely cripple and slow down their plans. It should buy us time to set up adequate protections and hopefully find out who is behind this and shut them down."

CHAPTER 48

July 16 - Monday

Miranda and Liz were relieved that there was a plan and hopefully an end to this madness.

They would tell their husbands as soon as they safely could relay the information without that unknown person or persons knowing what would be happening.

Miranda dropped Liz at her house and as she was pulling into her driveway, Kevin called and told her he was accepted into the finance internship position in London, England. He would be studying and working there all semester long. He would leave August first, fly to London and stay in apartments with his fellow students until December fifteenth. The program consisted of twenty internship hours a week and several courses to round out the educational component. A package with all the details would be coming in the mail within the next week.

Miranda began to plan immediately. They would have to make plane reservations, deal with the apartment lease and payments, books, tuition, transportation to and from work and the university and of course food. They would have just about two weeks to get his clothes together and make all the arrangements. Kevin would have to put in his notice to work, maybe he could work another week before quitting.

Miranda couldn't believe they only gave these kids a couple of weeks to make all of these arrangements. Or did Kevin just not tell her before now? Hopefully, the packet would provide phone numbers and checklists to help accomplish this. She decided she wasn't going to panic and just take it one day at a time. Kevin had to take most of the responsibility in making this happen.

Then the other shoe hit the floor. Erica came home from work that night and told Miranda that since Kevin was quitting soon she thought she might want to quit too. She had been thinking about the open tryouts for field hockey, which was why she started to run again to get back into shape. A number of her friends were going out and she thought she would too. She was convinced she had a very good chance of making the team.

Now Miranda felt overwhelmed. Not only did she have to deal with what was going on in Loveladies, she would have to orchestrate Kevin's move and get Erica ready to go back to school about the same time. She just hoped there wouldn't be a change to the time table on the purchase of the rental apartments. That was all she needed!

Would she stay down at the shore once they left or would she go back home and only come down on the weekends with Jack? She would have to talk with him about what would be best for the two of them.

Miranda spent most of the night talking with Jack about the kids' plans and how she was going to help them. She knew Jack wouldn't have the time to help other than on the weekends. Anything at this point would help. He might be able to get Kevin to the airport or help transport Erica's dorm room essentials and sports gear to her college.

Before hanging up, Miranda told Jack they would talk more over the weekend, there was so much to discuss with everything that was going on. She hoped he got the message. Maybe he would think to call John himself and get the update on the plan.

Alek listened to Miranda's conversations with her kids and Jack. She was going to be very busy the next few weeks, have to go home for an extended period and should be out of his hair.

CHAPTER 49

July 18 to 20 - Wednesday through Friday

The internship letter arrived at the shore house on Wednesday. Thankfully, Kevin had the foresight to have all the documents sent there instead of their home address. This just made things that much easier.

To her amazement, Miranda found the program specifics quite detailed and thorough. Apartments had already been arranged and Kevin was set with a roommate. Transportation to and from London's Heathrow was set up for arrival in August and departure in December. Vans were hired to take the students from their apartments to work or school and return them at the end of the day.

The only things Miranda needed to get done were money for food, spending and emergencies, clothing for school and work, and making sure his electronics had the appropriate adapter plugs. She couldn't remember from her past visit to England if she had to take that two plug system she and Jack bought for their trips to Europe. She would give them to Kevin either way just to make sure. Of course, he could just look up what he needed.

Kevin got Thursday off from work and he and Miranda left the island to do some shopping. Although there were many shops on and off the island they wouldn't have what he needed; they had to drive about forty-five minutes to Mays Landing to the Hamilton Mall. There was a Macy's there and even though Miranda hated to shop at Macy's because of the poor service she received in the past, it was better than driving all the way home. Of course, if they struck out on what he needed, they would still have to make the trip to the malls up there.

They were able to find two suits that would work for his internship, dress shoes, some new jeans, shirts and ties. He had enough clothes at home from his last school year to fill in what he needed. A quick lunch at Olive Garden and they were on their way back home. Miranda would have to check with Erica to see if she needed any new clothes for the coming year. She thought, *Oh! Silly me! What girl would say she did not need any new clothes? Maybe I will wait until she asks...*

Friday, Miranda received a call from Liz. Apparently, her interior decorator wanted her to come to her shop to go over some window treatment options on Saturday at eleven o'clock. Richard would be going; would Liz and Jack like to meet at eleven thirty at Buckalews in Beach Haven for lunch afterwards? Miranda got the hint and said they would love to. She called Jack and suggested he come down to the shore early on Saturday morning.

CHAPTER 50

July 18 - Wednesday

Alek found another report about the Oyster Creek shut-down. Exelon was outlining how they were going to proceed with the shut-down and the storage of the spent fuel rods. The public was concerned with the rods being stored on site because the company was only going to use armed guards and other undisclosed methods which seemed a bit under secured for the highly radioactive parts. The rods would be stored in wet pools for five years then moved to dry storage and eventually moved to an approved facility. Exelon had hoped for one particular facility but it had been defunded a few years ago so it was never completed. Oyster Creek would be shut down and defueling would finish by September thirtieth. The next step would be for the company to prepare for the 55 years of dormancy. *Whatever that meant.*

This would be interesting, thought Alek. *The spent nuclear fuel would be on site and only under armed guard?* Alek began searching other articles pertaining to spent nuclear fuel. *This website might provide some ideas* he thought as he began to read about fuel rods continuing to be radioactive and generating considerable heat for decades. To cool the rods down, they are put under about twenty feet of water, in a special pool, that was circulated to move the heated water away from the rods so they could maintain a safe temperature. Alek thought, '*Where does this circulated water go? Out in the bay? It would be hot and radioactive? I thought the closing of the site would help the bay heal, but it looks like the water quality won't improve until all those rods are cool. That will be years!*

The biggest issue they will have is if something happens to the water in these tanks. They have to be kept at a certain level. If the water level goes down or there is a leak or the cooling systems has a problem, the rods would heat what is left of the water causing it to boil and eventually evaporate. Then the rods would be exposed and heat to the point where they could rupture or burn thus causing a radiation leak. The more spent fuel rods they add to these cooling pools just increase the potential for problems. This could lead to Chernobyl types of problems.

So assuming nothing bad happens, these spent fuel rods have to spend five years in the pool until they are cool enough to move to the dry storage containers of steel and concrete.'

Alek began to think of possibilities. '*So anything we decide to do with the spent fuel would need to happen in the first five years while it is in the pools where it can cause the maximum of damage. The Nuclear Regulatory Commission had requirements and strategies to help prevent accidents and reduce damage from attacks but it really didn't seem like it would be sufficient.'*

Alek continued to search the internet for information. He found another article on spent nuclear fuel. He wondered when the last rods had been inserted in the reactor core, could any of them have had a short irradiation period. The short irradiation period made the plutonium in the rods bomb quality. The ones that had been used up in the reactor during normal operation were not. Did they date stamp them? Of course there would be records and some kind of coding on the rods that would tell the employees what they were dealing with. He continued to read on.

To protect these rods from terrorists and disasters like hurricanes and seiches, they had to be in a steel and concrete liner.

What the heck are seiches thought Alek.

He wondered if anything like this happened in New Jersey recently. Then he remembered that one summer, when there was that huge wave that hurt a few people in Barnegat Inlet. That was a seiche. He could see how a large wave like that could compromise those cooling pools.

If the cooling systems were damaged or the water evaporated or was somehow removed, the chances of a radiation leak were great. Also there were more fuel rods in the pools than in a reactor and they didn't have the same protection they would have inside the reactor.

So many possibilities, he thought. But what was he supposed to do about it? He would continue to research and be ready when the time came. The Exelon executive that he had been monitoring had provided him with some information, specifically the possibility they may sell the facility to another company. Once plans were in place to begin the decommission of the nuclear plant, he would have completed his research and be able to propose options to his superiors. This would be something for the long term, while the present surveillance will come to head by Labor Day. With any luck, there will be something that might allow the completion of both goals at once.

CHAPTER 51

July 21 - Saturday

Of course the meeting with the interior decorator was a ruse and John and Lori Franklin were at Buckalews waiting for the Craigs and the Goldbergs. They exchanged pleasantries while looking over the menu and ordering their lunch and drinks. Once the waitress left, John told them about the results from the autopsy and forensics.

"Initially, the preliminary results from the autopsy suggested food poisoning from the shellfish. And since no one had contacted Miranda or Jack about getting sick from the food on the Fourth of July, I suggested to the coroner to take a closer look. The toxicology screen came back as positive for Saxitoxin which is a neurotoxin associated with contaminated seafood. "

"However remote the chance that he ate the one piece of shellfish that poisoned him, they were clueless how it got into his system, and the amount in his system was more than what he would have gotten from his meal."

"Then yesterday, forensics got back the results on the traces of tobacco swept up from Frederick's floor and what was left in his cigarette pack. And guess what? The tobacco was laced with it. Now what makes this chemical interesting is its history with the military and the CIA and its purpose was for use as a biological or chemical weapon. All of it was supposed to be destroyed in the late 1960s but apparently some still exists. The big questions are: how was it obtained, by whom and why give it to Frederick."

The waitress returned with their food and drinks and all conversation momentarily stopped. They took a few minutes to eat and digest what John had told them.

Miranda asked John, "Will you please tell Richard and Jack what you told Liz and me on Monday at the library?"

"Of course, and we already have some information. As I told the women, we are running background checks on people in Loveladies to start. The occupations of people with summer homes here is quite interesting and impressive. We are finding people working for the power companies, transportation, law firms, banks, investment houses, the Security and Exchange Commission, FCC, phone companies, government positions, etc. So whoever is bugging these homes is looking for something very specific."

"Our agents will be going into residents' homes to fix internet issues caused by a fictitious power surge."

"We have secured the feed from all the residents that keep outside video recordings and they are being analyzed. The police told them we are looking for someone who stole some expensive tile from one of the construction sites. Since there are so many construction projects going on in this area, people just assume it is one on or near their street. They are willing to help."

"The two couples that Miranda and Jack met at Daymark at the beginning of the summer, their homes have been searched by the agents. It was very perceptive of them to notice the little things out of place in their homes. Their computers had spyware and their phones and home were bugged."

"We are discussing with Homeland Security and the Secret Service about methods to upload misleading documents and false updates to the various companies and agencies' systems so hackers have to re-do or update code and change their specs so that the final hack won't do anything. It has to be done without alerting them that we are on to them. We have people working around the clock on this and we still don't have an idea who is behind this and why. It could be a domestic terrorist; it could be like Miranda pointed out, the Russians. It could be hackers looking to profit financially from the data they mine, demanding a ransom. Regardless of who it is and why, we have to stop the hackers before they can take control. We have also been in contact with the Ukrainian government and the team that handled their data breach since this seems so similar to theirs. They were willing to share what they know and how they handled it. We hope this will give us some insight into what we are facing here."

No one had any additional observations to offer. Liz and Richard were very worried about what information might be gleaned from his laptop. He had Bill, his IT specialist, check what information was available, and was assured by him, no one could gain access into the company servers, client databases, employee emails, or Human Resource information. Richard wasn't convinced of this and asked John if they would work with his company also.

Jack thought for a moment then said, "Do you remember your history of World War II, when the Americans knew the Japanese were aiming their sights on one of the islands in the Pacific? They couldn't figure out which island was targeted by the Japanese code. The location was just AF. So they sent an uncoded message that Midway's water purification system was not working. Another Japanese message was intercepted that basically said that AF had a water problem. They knew the Japanese would be attacking Midway. "

"We need to come up with a message that is sent out to whomever from one of the bugged devices. It has to be so devastating or dangerous that it will require whoever it is to make a move. Like the way the Japanese identified Midway. Since we can't intercept their messages to see if they talk about the issue, we have to get them to act and act very openly; like they have to call the police or the fire department."

John thought about it for a moment then said, "I think that is very good idea, especially at this point when we don't know what we are up against. We can develop two scenarios where fictitious information is given stating major changes in the companies' operating systems or security and the other is something that will trigger an overt and highly visible reaction by whoever is doing this. In the meantime, I reiterate, that conversations are to be kept to a minimum in your homes and on the phones, until the agents can get to you. It should be fairly soon. I will try to expedite it. But as you can imagine, there are other systems these hackers have access to that are much more important than yours and therefore get priority treatment."

Miranda and Jack weren't as worried as Liz and Richard. There was nothing on their laptop and Jack never used it at home. Their phone conversations were limited and business was not discussed.

They settled up the tab and each couple started to leave to return to their homes. John turned to the rest of the group as they were getting into their cars and said, "Oh, one last thing. Miranda, you remember you asked me to check into Frederick's background? I haven't found anything yet, but this might be of interest to you. The medical examiner told me something thought-provoking about the autopsy of Frederick Wasserman that may indicate he was not Jewish as we once believed. He wasn't circumcised."

CHAPTER 52

July 21 - Saturday

Jack and Miranda didn't say much as they drove up the island. Traffic was getting heavier as people were coming off the beach and heading for home, a restaurant or to do some shopping. Miranda suggested they stop off at the Acme grocery store between Beach Haven Park and Brant Beach. Since they had a big lunch they could get away with something light. Maybe they could pick up some already prepared food. Miranda didn't really feel like cooking. In addition, they needed to discuss Kevin and Erica's plans and how they were going to get everything done.

Miranda and Jack had a quiet dinner that night. They just seemed to stare at each other, not knowing what to say. They eventually put on some music and opened another bottle of wine. They sang and danced around the great room and just generally enjoyed each other's company. Did they really need to talk? They seemed to be doing alright. It was almost like telepathy.

They had a strong marriage and family. Everyone worked hard at their particular positions. Everyone contributed and everyone gained. This particular bump in the road was just that. A bump. As with other hurdles they had faced in the past, they attacked each bump in the road head on. Miranda and Jack knew what each other was thinking. They would work with John and they would keep their eyes and ears open and do whatever they could. Two deaths on their lagoon were beyond belief.

They weren't a religious family. They didn't go to church or synagogue. They didn't believe in God, per se, but believed in a higher power. Something influenced the world. They believed they could influence the world by doing the right thing, by helping others and actively searching out others to help. They didn't look down on religion, just didn't find it fit their beliefs. Everyone made their peace somehow and found their solace somewhere.

Chicky Haverford had his family to look out for him and fight for justice. Frederick had no one. Miranda and Jack knew they had to help him find peace. They also had to do it for themselves and their family. Miranda had a feeling Liz and Richard felt the same way. There were the other people and families that had been impacted by this invasion of privacy and that had to end too.

Maynard had to go outside, so Miranda and Jack went out with him. They stood on the dock while he did his business and wondered around the backyard. The night was so peaceful and beautiful. This was a true Loveladies evening. The night sky was loaded with stars, the moon shined brightly over their house. Thankfully, the neighbors on the lagoon had their outdoor lights off so no ambient light interfered with the show. They took their glasses of wine and lay down on the outdoor couches and just stared up at the sky. If they were lucky, they would see a few shooting stars. The real star show would be in the middle of August when the Perseid Meteor Shower would reach over fifty meteors an hour. Some past years, there had been twice that many.

Maynard lay down on the teak tiles beside the couch, content to be outside with his family. The kids came home and found everyone outside. They quickly showered, changed into comfortable, warmer clothes, and joined Miranda, Jack and Maynard watching the night sky. They found Loveladies ennui whenever and wherever possible. And this was a classic.

When Miranda heard snoring coming from the kids, Jack and the dog, she knew it was time to move the herd inside.

CHAPTER 53

July 22 - Sunday

Miranda was determined to continue the feeling from the previous night. Being a Sunday, there would be no construction and hopefully no neighborhood noise. Since they were outside for most of the night, everyone was sleeping in, even Maynard.

Counting her blessings, she crept around the house so as not to wake anyone up, especially the dog. She made her instant coffee and went outside. With her heavy robe and slippers, she was comfortable enough to be in the cool morning air for a period of time. She went back to the outdoor couch and lay down, reliving the night before. Now the sky was light blue with wispy clouds.

It was almost six and the only sound Miranda could hear were the waves crashing on the beach to the east. The sun was barely up, there was some brightness just over the tree line to her right.

She decided to move to the couch by the dock line and lay down again. She heard a noise coming from her left and moved up slightly to see what it was. She saw Alek coming down the winding staircase from the upper level of his house. He had his cooler in one hand and what looked like an old fashioned cell phone in the other.

She scrunched down further on the couch so he couldn't see her. She found him so creepy and mysterious. *'Why in the world would someone go out everyday fishing at six in the morning?'* wondered Miranda. *Did they not have enough money for dinner? Gee, what a stupid question. Just think how much fuel costs for his excursions! You could buy…who knows what! They measure boat fuel consumption by how many gallons are burned by the hour. And it is not 1 gallon. He probably uses about ten gallons per hour at four dollars a gallon going to his fishing site then his return. Fuel at the marinas is expensive. When they followed him out, they traveled for about an hour one way. It would cost him eighty dollars a day, all for eight dollars' worth of fish. So what was he up to?*

Alek loaded his gear on the boat then went back inside. He came out again and just stood on his dock and looked around. This wasn't the first time Miranda saw him do this. He stood there for a good five minutes just looking around. Then he seemed to focus on her house. Did he see her? She immediately ducked her head down to make sure she was invisible to him. She was able to still see him by peeking between the back cushions. He could have seen her come out earlier and was wondering where she was.

Eventually, he turned and walked over to his boat and removed the lines from the pilings. Jumping on, he moved to his weatherproof pilot house and started his boat. As he pulled away, his eyes never left the back of the couch where Miranda lay. He must have known she was there.

It seemed like hours passed before she felt safe to sit up and make sure he was gone. She went inside and woke Jack up.

"Jack, wake up!" Miranda whispered into Jack's ear. "I just had the weirdest experience outside. I was lying on the couch enjoying my coffee and the beautiful morning and Alek came out. I didn't think he could see me; I had been out there awhile. But he kept staring in my direction. My Spidey senses are tingling. There really is something up with him. I think we need to ask John to focus the background checks and scans on him; if only just to rule him out or to find out if he, too, has been bugged or hacked."

"I have been thinking about what John told us. Loveladies, and even the island, is such a microcosm of the whole Eastern Seaboard. People have homes here from all over, wealth that has been built from a wide range of occupations. Occupations that are important to the everyday functioning of our world. Someone is taking advantage of what we do and what we know for some nefarious reason. Just the way Alek was looking over here, I felt threatened. I know it sounds crazy, but I was really frightened."

Jack pulled Miranda down onto the bed beside him and cradled her in his arms whispering back, "After breakfast, let's take a walk over to John's house and we can ask him to please take a closer look at Alek."

About nine thirty, Miranda began making French toast and bacon for breakfast. The coffee was brewing and the aromas were permeating around the house. She knew that would get the kids up.

She put up an umbrella at the outdoor table, and placed the dishes around on placemats. Making a meal visually appealing always made it taste even better. The kids wondered out and sat down, big smiles on their faces as they poured hot maple syrup on the stacks of French toast and crispy bacon.

Miranda couldn't help but smile. She had to enjoy this, they would both be gone in a few weeks and she would see very little of them until the middle of December. What would she do when they graduate, get jobs and move away? Or heaven forbid not be able to find a job and continue to live at home? They seemed to notice the look on her face, and uncharacteristically they each touched her hand and said "Thanks for a great breakfast Mom!" and then they laughed and started wolfing down their food. So much for sentimentality.

The kids left to do something; she really hadn't paid attention to what their plans were for the day. She thought she heard they worked in the afternoon until seven that night.

The dishes could wait until after the conversation with John. Miranda thought she should call Liz and tell her what they were doing, but couldn't figure out how to say it and not give away the real purpose to whomever was eavesdropping. She would have to fill her in later.

As they were walking over to the Franklin's Jack said, "Miranda, I think it would be best if the kids quit their jobs soon and all of you come home for a while. I am getting a bad feeling about all of this too. There is so much to get done and I can help more if all of you are up North. Then hopefully, after Kevin leaves for London and Erica returns to school, the authorities will have cleared this whole mess up and we can get on with our lives."

"Jack, I agree. I would feel much safer at home than down here. After we speak with John, I will let Liz know what my plan is. I think it would be wise if she did the same thing. At least we could communicate openly."

When they got over to the Franklin's they found only Lori home. She explained that John was following up on some leads and wouldn't be back for a day or two. They explained what they wanted John to know and Lori promised to pass along the information.

Kevin and Erica were just leaving for work as Jack and Miranda were walking down their street. They stopped the car and rolled down their window, "Hey, we will see you about seven fifteen. What's for dinner?"

Miranda said, "It is a surprise. Kids, there has been a change in plans. Please tell Antonio that you need to stop work on Tuesday and we are going home on Wednesday to get things ready for the school year."

Erica started to complain, "But Mom, I wanted to make at least another five days of pay before going home!"

"There is no discussion of this, and apologize to him for having to leave earlier than you had planned. Dad and I will tell you more after we get home on Wednesday."

CHAPTER 54

July 22 - Sunday

Alek steered his boat down the lagoon after being out on the ocean all day. Not only was he able to retrieve a message canister and set afloat another with downloaded data for the hackers, he even caught a fish for dinner.

As he approached his dock, his wife came out to help tie up the boat to the pilings. She took the coolers he handed to her and went inside to start dinner for the two of them.

He sprayed down his boat, cleaned out the live well after removing his fish then stepped off to clean his catch at his outdoor sink.

Looking across the lagoon at the Craig's house he remembered seeing the Craig woman spying on him while trying to hide behind the cushions on the outdoor couch. She must suspect him of something otherwise why would she be acting so strange and constantly watching his comings and goings. She and her husband had gotten pretty chummy with that Franklin fellow over on the next street, who just so happens to be in law enforcement. Too bad he had all those cameras and a very sophisticated security alarm on his house; otherwise, he would have broken in and bugged the house, phones and computers.

Thank goodness, everything was almost complete. Just a few more weeks were needed by the hackers to complete all the coding to take over the various facilities. He would be able to trigger the malware to self-destruct with no trace remaining. Everything would take place at once. He would have to be extra careful and keep a closer eye on his neighbors.

He took the filleted fish into the house and handed it to his wife. She finished up dinner while he took a quick shower.

As she was putting the food on the table, Alina said, "It is such a shame Frederick died. I was just talking with Ruth Weinstein at the Foundation today. She and I got to reminiscing about the old days when we all moved down here and the fun we had at all those parties the Silvermasters used to have. We used to enjoy our neighbors so much. We all loved the arts and there was so much talent down here. Then the psychologists and psychiatrists came, Frederick among them. There was drinking and other forms of 'relaxation', political discussions and the music. We were all free spirits; but now, not so much. It is just so sad. Ruth even mentioned that after you started working for Silvermaster and Ullmann, you really changed and we began to distance ourselves from the others. I supposed it was all the hard construction work you were doing and were too tired to socialize. But after Nathan got you that job with the think tank, we should have tried harder to get back in the group again. Although, I never really cared for the Haverfords and Chicky was always asking me questions about you, especially last year. I never told you because I didn't want you to be upset about him bothering me."

Alek started thinking to himself, *Maybe that was why Frederick had always worked hard to maintain the friendship; to keep close tabs on him. He hadn't known what Chicky had been up to talking with his wife, she couldn't have told him much could she? Maybe it was because she was so elusive? Or had it been his initial working relationship with Silvermaster and Ullmann that fed Chicky's curiosity over the years? Being in the CIA, he would have ways of keeping an eye on him. It was a good thing I killed him when I did. Now, I just have to find out if Frederick kept any documentation on their suspicions.*

CHAPTER 55

July 25 - Wednesday

The kids finished up work on Tuesday, said goodbye to all their friends and promised to keep in touch over the school year. With Facebook, Twitter and Instagram, it was easy to update everyone where they were, what they were doing, what they were eating and who they were with just with a click and a simple keystroke or post. They would swing by the deli on their way home on Wednesday and pick up their last paychecks.

Miranda had called Liz and told her their plans and was hoping to be back at the shore no later than August sixth. Liz, too, had plans to return home for a while and would let Miranda know when she would come back down. They agreed to talk more in the next few days from home, knowing they would be able to communicate more freely.

The kids had packed up everything they had at the shore and would sort through it at home to determine what they would need for the coming months. Miranda had to pack up more than she normally would since she would be home for almost two weeks. She wouldn't take any food home, what was at the shore would be alright until she returned. She would however have to go to the store immediately when she got home, sure that there was nothing in the refrigerator or pantry. She had cleaned out most of what was there and had brought it to the shore for Memorial Day. Of course, the kids had put in their requests for special dinners for the remaining nights before heading back to school.

Tonight, it would be Chicken Francaise over linguine with sautéed broccoli and garlic. This was a family favorite, everyone loving the lemony sauce over the pasta, but it was such a pain in the neck to make. She would have to make extra chicken so they would be able to make sandwiches with it tomorrow for lunch.

After dinner, Miranda and Jack told Kevin and Erica what they had been told by John about Frederick and Chicky deaths and the number of houses that had been bugged. They did not tell them how Homeland Security and the Secret Service were uncovering the residents, only that they had a plan to resolve the problem. If the kids posted anything on social media, there was no telling who had access and it would not help to forewarn the hackers.

The rest of the night was spent planning what had to be done in the next few days and who was going to do what. Clothes had to be washed and folded, suitcases gotten out of the attic, Erica's car needed an oil change and the brakes and tires needed to be checked. Thankfully, Kevin had updated his passport two years ago when a friend had invited him to Bermuda for spring break, so there wouldn't be a mad rush or expense to have a new one expedited. Miranda wondered if they should go to the American Express office to pick up some Travelers' Checks or just have him use a credit card.

CHAPTER 56

July 27 - Friday

Alek knew he had to get into Frederick's homes and office again. A more thorough search was needed to locate his files. He didn't think the police had been successful; otherwise they would have come to question him. He was sure there was something in those documents that would implicate him based on what Chicky had intimated last Labor Day.

After telling his wife that he would be gone for about week at a conference sponsored by the think tank, he packed up a bag of clothing and another with tools he would need once he got to Frederick's properties. He wanted to make sure he had enough time to accomplish whatever needed to be done. If he found the files early, he would simply tell her that the remaining days were not of interest to him.

Having gained entrance once to Frederick's home and office, he was sure he would not have any problems this time. It had been a few weeks since Frederick's death, and he hoped there would be no police presence there.

He drove to the office first and parked in the garage. He grabbed the ticket at the entrance and looked around for any cameras that might record his license plate. This was an old building in a decent area so the management company, thankfully, didn't feel the need for monitoring devices or were just too cheap to install them. Alek noticed there weren't too many cars on the level where he parked and he hoped this was a sign that many employees from the building were taking vacation time.

Exiting the elevator on Frederick's floor, he saw the hallway was empty and there was still police tape crossing the office doorway. He thought to himself, *'Do they really think that will stop someone from entering?'*

He put on a pair of latex gloves and used his instruments to unlock the door and gently removed a piece of the tape so he could enter. Securing the tape back into place, he closed the door and turned on the interior light. It was obvious the police had conducted a thorough search of the premises but there was no evidence of any remaining files. Could they have found them? Frederick had been practicing psychiatry for many years and there should be boxes or crates of files and records. He had to keep them somewhere secure, and the search of his financial records showed that he didn't use a record storage facility, safety deposit box or a self-storage locker. He couldn't imagine where else he could keep them.

Thinking about his own situation, Alek began to explore the bookcases to see if they moved and paneling to see if there were any hidden areas. He searched for hours, checking under the rugs, in the chair and couch cushions, for secret panels in the desk, behind paintings and photographs, and he even checked the tank on the back of the toilet. There were no files, keys, invoices or notes that would indicate another location that could be a hiding place.

Turning off the lights, he slowly opened the door and removed the section of tape. Much to his dismay, when he tried to secure it on the door frame, it wouldn't stick. He would just have to leave it dangling. Luckily the elevator opened as soon as he hit the down button. Returning his bag to the trunk of his car, he got in and headed to Frederick's house twenty minutes away.

He would need to be more careful here. It was a busy little neighborhood, cars constantly going up and down the street, kids on bikes, joggers and walkers heading toward the park. Sitting in his car about seventy-five feet away, Alek decided he would have to come back when it was dark. There would be no way he could try to get in without being seen.

After having a meal at one of the local restaurants near Frederick's home, he parked his car the next block over and waited until nightfall. Gathering the few tools he thought he would need, he cautiously walked to the house. Just on a whim, he checked the mailbox and was rewarded with a stack of letters, large envelopes and one package.

Everything was quiet on the street as he walked to the backyard and entered through the door off the garage. He would search the garage after he went over every inch inside the little bungalow.

First, he thought, maybe I should just take a look at the mail, maybe get lucky. Water, electric, property and sewer tax reminder, waste removal, phone bill, and a bunch of junk mail. The large confidential envelope contained a few session notes and reports, but nothing of consequence. He did notice the name of the transcription service. It was strange that Frederick would have the reports sent to his home. Maybe he had reduced his patient load with his advanced age and it was easier and more convenient to have the reports sent here to the house. If he was unlucky in searching the properties, he might have to take a look at the transcription service.

He stuffed the mail into his pack and continued with his search. He methodically went room to room, searching top to bottom, looking in obvious and odd places. There were no hidden rooms, spaces or compartments and no files. There was no computer or laptop, which he already surmised by Frederick's lack of technical skills.

The garage, his last location to check proved equally barren. He went back to his car and pulled out his cell phone. He plugged in the transcription service name and found the address. It was only a few miles away. Now would be a perfect time to check it out.

Following his GPS directions, Lincoln Technical and Medical Transcription Service was located in a strip mall at the edge of town. It was a very small office with only one desk inside. That would make sense, to limit the number of people listening and transcribing his notes. They would have to insure the utmost in confidentiality to physicians and psychiatrists. He wondered why Chicky wouldn't have him use the services available through the CIA unless they weren't working under the auspices of the agency. Or could this little business be a front for operatives to pass along information right out in the open?

He observed a woman sitting at the desk typing. Office hours were posted on the front door clearly showing a Monday through Friday business. Being outside normal business hours he thought this strange, but then reasoned since there was only one desk, she might be overworked and thus had to stay late to keep up with her work load. He would wait until tomorrow night to investigate this location hoping she wouldn't be there.

The next night, Alek again parked his car far enough away that it wouldn't be spotted. He found the back entrance to the office and was able to pick the lock on the door without any problems. He took out his little pen light and began looking around the office. There were a few filing cabinets, but after searching the drawers, found no files or invoices. Apparently, they had everything computerized and in their system. There were reams of paper, envelopes, and a few other office supply items. The desk contained similar items along with a few flash drives. The only thing of interest to him was the computer and he didn't think it wise to spend too much time in an office with large windows in the front. So, he took the processor and the flash drives and left. He would try to access what records they had on the computer.

CHAPTER 57

July 28 through August 10

Miranda sat alone at the dining room table with her cold cup of coffee, staring out at the backyard. This house was so different from the shore; there was no view of the neighbors, no water and absolutely no activity other than a bird or squirrel in the trees. The only sound was the clock ticking on the wall of the kitchen. There was so much to get done in a short period of time. All she could think about was the shore and trying to figure out who was interested in all those residents and why.

John had called and spoken with Miranda and Jack, saying Jersey City Power and Light was going to shut down the power next Friday night for one hour from seven until eight. Then at eight o'clock, the cable companies and internet providers were shutting down all service on the island.

Teams of agents and technicians would begin their rounds on Saturday and emails would be sent out from the various property owner associations and the township. The residents would hopefully see the emails on their cell phones.

Of those residents identified so far, plans had been put in place with their employers to begin correspondence via snail mail and fax about necessary changes to the company systems, thus throwing a monkey wrench into the plans of the hackers. The IT specialists within these companies were changing critical operating systems so that whatever hack was being initiated wouldn't work. Security systems were being upgraded.

After conducting the remaining searches and identifying any other potential hackees, the federal agents would move on to the next phase of the operation.

The critical part of the mission was to identify the individual or individuals that were responsible for initiating this hack. John made it clear to Miranda and Jack when he called them that Homeland Security, the NSA and the Secret Service were certain this was the same group that attacked the Ukraine a few years back. The hackers' intent was to disrupt and destroy as much as possible, hopefully bringing America to its knees. The U.S. Government had been aware that we were being targeted and had teams working to uncover operatives and networks. But they had been unsuccessful until Miranda stumbled on the malware and bugging in Loveladies. Knowing who was targeted gave the government something to work with and now the main focus was tracking the hackers down and securing the systems.

John had spent most of this time since they last spoke working up a dossier on Alek Pronin, and the more he researched the more he found he might be a logical candidate. But at this point it was merely conjecture.

He told them of his Communist background, his father's work as a Russian Ambassador and how Alek had even worked construction in Loveladies helping to build many of the homes when he was much younger.

Now he was employed with a think tank that was believed to have ties to Russia. Again, this was not enough to convict him, but enough to warrant further investigation and make him a prime suspect.

Jack accompanied the family to Newark Airport to see Kevin off for London. They had been able to get everything done, all the clothes packed in two large suitcases. If Kevin needed anything else, he could just buy it there. It was an emotional send off, with all that had been going on. There were lots of hugs and kisses and promises of pictures and Face Timing. Even though she was sad, Miranda was quite excited for Kevin and the opportunities he would have living abroad for a few months.

Now they just had to get Erica squared away and drive her to school on Sunday.

Saturday, John called again with another update,

"Agents have been working on Liz and Alek's street, and for your information, Liz and Richard's home is cleared now. We will be clearing your house in a few days. Alek's wife would not let the agents into the home, saying her husband was away on business and they would have to wait until he returned. Just looking in the house from the front door showed no computer or laptop, but they are receiving service from Comcast on the island for television and internet. She told the agents that her husband was at a conference for his work and expected him to return by the end of next week. The agents agreed to follow up Thursday or Friday."

"His background is quite interesting and leads us to believe he could be involved. We just don't know how."

Sunday came quite quickly, too quickly for Miranda. She and Jack helped Erica load her car with what she thought she would need for the next few months. They would have to put some items, like her mini refrigerator and book case in Miranda's Ford Explorer. It seemed like each year Erica took more items for her small room. Miranda just couldn't see where it all would go. She dreaded unloading the car at school. They always had to park in the lot and carry arm loads at least one hundred feet to the door, wait for Erica to swipe in, and then either wait for the elevator or climb three flights of stairs. It would be an exhausting day. And of course, Erica would want to grab some dinner before they headed back, inviting a number of friends to join them. They wouldn't be able to stay too long, Maynard would need to be fed and let outside since they left him at home.

When they were finally on their way home, Jack told Miranda that he had gotten a voice mail message from their lawyer while at dinner. Jack put it on speaker phone. "Hi Jack and Miranda; its Phil Bennett here. Sorry for calling you on a Sunday at this hour, but I had to tell you the closing on the apartment building is scheduled for Wednesday, August eighth. I hope that doesn't mess up any plans you have for the week, but the seller all of sudden is anxious to get this deal over with. I need both of you there for the closing. Let me know if this is a problem, otherwise, I will just see you at my office at ten o'clock. So long."

Miranda would need to stay home until after the papers were finalized. She didn't have a problem with this and was quite relieved that she wouldn't have to be at the shore when the agents were making their rounds. When she finally got down there, hopefully everything would be taken care of and the perpetrator caught.

They made plans for the rest of the week after the closing, and Jack decided he would take Friday off and each would drive down in the morning. They would try for a nice relaxing weekend; possibly get together with the Goldmans and the Franklins if they were around. They would have been away just over two weeks and wondered what the Haverford house would look like.

Still in Philadelphia trying to figure out his next steps, Alek found a library where he could check on news concerning Oyster Creek. He plugged in his search criteria and was rewarded with a number of articles. He chose the first one and it appeared to be a press announcement from a company that specialized in managing and decommissioning reactors. They were hoping the deal to buy Oyster Creek from Exelon would go through in the third quarter of 2019. Regulatory approval was required and they would be taking over the entire holdings and process- the site, buildings, handling and disposing of the used nuclear fuel and finally restoring the site. They proposed to complete the entire project within eight years with the help of another company. The release also mentioned they were waiting on a license for an interim storage facility in New Mexico for the spent nuclear fuel. A trust fund had been set up many years ago to take care of the costs involved with the shut down and decommissioning of the site, so when the deal goes through, if it went through, this new company would get its hands on a lot of money.

When he was done with the article, Alek did a quick search and found it was a private company with operations in four states, a number of countries in Europe, South America and Ukraine. The Ukraine, how fortunate. He would have to contact his superiors to see what information they might have garnered from their previous hacks in the Ukraine.

Alek decided he would put together a brief report of his findings while still at the library and return home on Thursday.

Miranda met Jack at the attorney's office on Wednesday. The seller and his attorney arrived on time at ten and the group got down to business. Jack had made the deposit on the property and those funds were held in escrow by the title agent. They had created a limited liability corporation as the legal owner of the apartment building. This way, if they got sued for whatever reason, they wouldn't lose any of their personal assets, only that of the investment, thus limiting their liability. Plus, there were the tax benefits. They brought the necessary documents to prove they had the authority to sign the contracts for the LLC. Prior to the closing, they had met with their attorney to go over the sales contract, title insurance, surveys of the property, the remaining rental leases of the tenants, environmental reports, zoning, taxes and a number of other items.

So with all the closing documents reviewed and agreed upon, they signed and became the proud owners of an apartment building. This would be quite an undertaking and Miranda was looking forward to the challenge. They had agreed to retain the existing property manager for several months until they had a chance to figure how involved they wanted to be in the day to day management of the property.

Having accomplished the monumental tasks of getting Kevin to London, Erica to school for field hockey tryouts and closing on the apartments, it was time to celebrate. Miranda and Jack tossed a coin to see if they would eat Italian or Thai. She was relieved that Thai won. They had eaten so much Italian food down at the shore she was frankly quite sick of it.

They went to one of their favorite restaurants in Basking Ridge. They always seemed to settle on the same menu items each time they were there; starting with the Peking Duck Salad that had apples, pineapple, nuts and a spicy dressing. Then, they would share the steamed mussels in a lemongrass and Thai basil broth. Finally, as the main course, spicy wild boar tenderloins with basil, mushrooms, bok choy and sticky rice. Of course, Jack had thought ahead and brought a bottle of wine knowing this was a BYOB restaurant.

Friday morning, they got up early, loaded their cars and headed for the shore, Maynard riding with Miranda. She had phoned Liz and arranged for them to meet at Black Eyed Susan's in Harvey Cedars for dinner that night. They were eager to catch up and make plans for the rest of the summer.

When Miranda, Jack and Maynard walked into their house, they saw a note on the table from John Franklin stating they had been through the house on Wednesday and cleaned out every device they could find. He would try to be in touch in the next few days but he and the agents were very busy, as Miranda and Jack could imagine.

With a sigh of relief, they unloaded their cars. It was going to be a beautiful day and Jack was anxious to go out on his boat. Miranda, just wanted to sit and enjoy some solitude and relaxation. Maybe even finish her book out by the pool.

They both went outside to check on the progress of the Haverford house. It was hard to believe the amount of work that had been completed in just over two weeks. The pool was in as was most of the landscaping. The exterior of the house looked finished with the exception of a few missing trim areas. They imagined the inside was far from complete, knowing that tile, carpet, furniture, painting and finish carpentry were the last things on the list before the homeowners would move in. There were still the sounds of saws, hammers and men talking but not at the decibels of the previous month. Maybe the summer was not a complete loss!

CHAPTER 58

August 9 - Thursday

Alek returned home to find his wife, Alina quite agitated. Apparently, she had been trying to reach him while he was away and she was very angry with him for not answering his phone, listening to his messages or returning her calls. Some men came to the house saying there had been a power outage that may have caused some damage to their electronics. The television hadn't worked since Friday night and she was trying to ask him what she should do. She was not comfortable letting someone in the house when he wasn't there, but now that he had returned he could deal with it.

Immediately, Alek sensed something was wrong with the situation. He excused himself and went to his office to check out his equipment. Nothing seemed to be wrong, other than he had no internet connection. This was problematic because he would be unable to monitor the targets' devices. If there was a problem with the cable and internet would he be able to get it fixed without letting them into this room or have access to his systems?

He thought maybe he could find out something if he checked on some of the bugs. Maybe he could find out what was going on and how wide scale these problems were. But when he tried to listen in on a number of locations, he heard nothing. These devices shouldn't be impacted by a power outage. He checked each and every location, nothing. Maybe it was more than a power outage like an electromagnetic pulse.

Just then, the doorbell rang. He heard his wife answer it and yell to him that the men were back about the cable.

He came out of his office and greeted the men asking to see their employee badges. After showing their Comcast credentials, they proceeded to tell him that they were back on his street again and thought they would stop by to see if he had returned home early. They told him this was an island wide outage and they were doing their best to rectify the situation as fast as possible. Had the wife let them in last week, this would have been cleared up already. They just needed access to the cable box, modem, router and any computer or laptop in the house. Many people had complained that their laptops were not functioning after the surge when the power came back on.

Luckily, everything but the computers/laptops was in the living room by the television. He informed them he did not have the laptop here at this time; he had left it with an associate at the conference he attended before the power went therefore it would not be affected.

The technicians went about their repair work. Alek would have to wait until they were done to see if his computers were damaged and if so he would have to fix them himself.

Hearing this was an island wide issue, he was greatly concerned. Would he still have access to all those people and their data? How could something like this happen?

After they left an hour later, he again turned on his computers and attempted to sign on. This time it worked. He checked his email for the messages the technician mentioned. Yes, they were there from the Loveladies Harbor Organization, Loveladies Property Owners Association and Long Beach Township.

Next, he thought he should check on some of the computers he had been monitoring to see if they were functioning. On the first one, he accessed their email and saw the same emails he just read on his computer. Then he saw emails from this particular person's company outlining new security protocols, new updates and instructions on uploading data fixes. Everything he had previously sent to his hackers had been changed. He tried to access this person's company servers and was shut down.

Panicking, he tried another computer. He found the same thing- no access and major fixes across the board with the company.

He started to systematically check on all the computers. The same result each time- no access and major changes to all systems. How was he going to re-tap all these homes, install new malware and get it to the hackers in time for the Labor Day deadline? How did they find out about his breach? How did they all respond so quickly and make the changes in time to stop him?

He would have to inform his superiors and await further instructions. He began to compose an encrypted message and included the information about Oyster Creek. He would leave as soon as possible to make his drop in the Atlantic.

CHAPTER 59

August 10 - Friday

While Alek awaited a response from his latest report, he checked the internet again for any changes with Oyster Creek. Another article was posted.

Oh, this just keeps getting better and better, thought Alek. *We might not have to do one thing, because the way it is playing out, it should be a disaster all on its own! This new company, if they get the go ahead on the sale, plans to use its own dry storage casks for the used nuclear fuel once it has cooled sufficiently. Some of the casks had malfunctioned in California and at another facility, they found additional problems. Also this company wants to open a location in New Mexico to store the waste which would require them to transport this radioactive material across the country. This could be very interesting, there are quite a few states between New Jersey and New Mexico. Would they allow these casks to be transported that many miles out in the open?*

Alek continued to read there was another company involved in the process that faced criminal charges in Canada.

Not only were there concerns about the reputability of these three companies, they would also be given the decommissioning fund which turned out to be close to one billion dollars.

Alek pondered the possibilities. *If we can't use the spent fuel rods for anything, or we can't create a radioactive disaster, maybe we could get our hands on that billion dollars?*

CHAPTER 60

August 13 through August 17 - Monday-Friday

Feeling relieved that the bugs had been removed and they could finally get back to normal, Miranda spent most of the week trying to catch up on all the housework and gardening that had been neglected while they were up North. It was astonishing how fast weeds grew in the yard and garden. Not only that, with the salt and moisture in the air, the bathroom showers and toilets were petri dishes for all sorts of mold, mildew and who knew what. It would do her good to do some scrubbing and pulling and taking out her aggressions on some inanimate objects.

By Friday night, the house was clean, the yard and the garden were weed free and producing tomatoes, cucumbers and figs. She would pick a basket full and take some to Liz for the weekend. There would be plenty for the dinners she was preparing for Jack on Saturday and Sunday night.

Miranda felt good and thought she deserved a reward. She opened a bottle of white wine, some Sancerre Jack had purchased just for her, knowing it was a favorite wine region of hers. She would drink her wine and watch a movie in the back room. It was a beautiful cool night. She had the sliding glass doors open and Maynard was asleep on the couch.

She began to overhear the Haverford's talking on their almost completed back porch. The wife was complaining about the "fucking landscapers" and the "workmen from Seattle that had had fucked up their ceiling."

Miranda hearing this got off the couch and moved to the back corner of the room by the last sliding glass door. This location of the house was like a little alcove for sound to bounce off from across the lagoon. She couldn't believe how well she could hear their conversation. If Liz could only see her now! She would never hear the end of it.

"And then I get this letter addressed to your father from that asshole Dr. Wasserman. On the envelope is says 'Upon my death, please deliver to Warner Haverford. It is from some attorney in Philadelphia. Inside, there is some quote…" Just then a car drove by and Miranda couldn't quite make out what she was saying.

"John Steinbeck. <u>The Grapes of Wrath,</u>" continued her neighbor. What the fuck am I supposed to do with this message? Wasserman is dead, he meant nothing to us. I'm just going to throw it away."

Miranda couldn't believe what she was hearing. First, boy that woman was a piece of work. She always seemed so hoity toity, but man she could talk like a long haul trucker. Second, this could be important. It was a message, possibly some kind of code meant specifically for Chicky. She was unable to get any part of the quote but thought possibly Diane could help at the library; they would be able to write the whole thing down and try to figure out what it might mean.

She called Liz to tell her about it. Liz had dashed home for a few days but would be down no later than next Wednesday. She also called Jack and told him.

CHAPTER 61

August 17 - Friday

Alek had taken the canister with the note out to a spot in the ocean not far from his favorite fishing spot last Friday. He returned every day waiting for a response. If his superiors had responded, his GPS device would alert him to the coordinates of a canister in the water. He desperately needed instructions; he didn't know what to do.

Finally, Friday morning he went out as always, leaving at about six as usual. As he was exiting the Barnegat Inlet, his GPS emitted a signal and coordinates were displayed where he could find the canister with a response. Having found the exact location, he fished it out with his net. He would have to wait until he got home to decipher the message.

It took a while to decode the message, but it was specific. He had to find a way to get back into those homes and specific targets were suggested as priorities.

Secondly, they had a mole in the CIA who had access to some of the reports of the current investigation on the island. The authorities, mainly the CIA, were still trying to find Frederick's letters and reports. They were aware Chicky and Frederick were on to something but they hadn't passed along their suspicions. Agents had been tearing apart all the properties but coming up empty handed. Alek's other priority was to uncover and destroy those reports. He had to get them before the CIA got their hands on them. There was no telling what they contained.

And finally, continue to monitor the Oyster Creek progress and submit observations, ideas and research findings as soon as possible.

What Miranda didn't know, was that Alek had re-bugged her house after the agent had cleared everything away. He heard her telephone conversation with Liz Goldberg and he knew exactly what Frederick was implying. His old friend had written that message before Chicky's death but had never informed the attorney to send it to someone else later on. It would tell him where the evidence was hidden. He knew the title was more important than the quote.

Alek would have to get the documentation before Miranda had a chance to tell John Franklin. He would have to take care of the dog tomorrow and her tomorrow night. Maybe the raccoon would return if he couldn't find another way to lure her outside at night.

CHAPTER 62

August 17-19 - Friday through Sunday

The Craigs had spent quite a lot of time outside on Friday night. Jack had been able to get away early from the office and they were enjoying a leisurely meal out on the deck, then wine out on their couches. Alek saw the couple outside and assumed Jack would be around for the weekend. He didn't think it would be safe to sneak out of his house until late Sunday night and to scatter various food items around the Craig's backyard. He needed to wait until the husband would be gone, so that she would have to deal with the dog alone.

He had read online that chocolate was really bad for dogs as were grapes and tomatoes. Since George had grapes in his yard and the Craigs had tomatoes, they would assume that birds had picked them and dropped them into the yard. He had purchased a number of different types of candy bars with nuts, milk chocolate and dark chocolate. Kids could have thrown them over the fence. All he had to do was wait for the dog to gorge himself on the 'treats' he put out. He didn't know if eating these items would kill the dog, but he really didn't care. That dog had been a pain in his neck for years, always barking at him when he would be outside. Then once the dog was taken care of, he would be able to take care of her and her husband if need be.

The Craigs spent most of the day Saturday and Sunday outside reading, swimming and relaxing. With their kids gone and the Goldbergs not at the shore this weekend, they really had very little to do.

Finally, while they were outside on Sunday Alek overhead Jack say to Miranda, "I think I better go home tonight. I have another early morning client meeting tomorrow and I am worried about getting stuck in traffic if I go home Monday morning. I hope you don't mind. I will try to get as much work done in the next few days so I can come back maybe Wednesday or Thursday."

"I understand," said Miranda. "I am exhausted after being out in the sun all day and will probably go to bed early anyway. I also want to go the library first thing tomorrow and work with Diane on the quote and then try to reach John and talk to him about the letter the Haverfords received."

Jack went into the bedroom, packed up his clothes and briefcase and left.

Miranda grabbed a bath towel, washcloth and robe and went to get cleaned up for bed in the outdoor shower. When she spent a lot of time outside during the day, she preferred to shower outside. Plus, she needed to check to see if there was enough soap and shampoos to last to the end of summer. Jack always preferred the outdoor shower and she needed to make sure he had what he needed.

The outdoor shower was basically another room off the side of the house. It had a bench to sit on, hooks to put your towel and robe and a nice big area under the shower nozzle. She generally stocked up on supplies at the beginning of the summer but with the kids and their friends using this shower after going to the beach, the cleaning products went faster than expected. She also noted that there were some spider webs and some mold growing in the corners. She would have to bring some bleach out with her tomorrow night when she showered so she could clean it out.

After her shower, she decided she would just crawl into bed and watch some TV until she fell asleep. Maynard had been out all day and would surely be tired too.

CHAPTER 63

August 19 - Sunday

Alek saw Jack leave and later saw Miranda take her shower and then go into their bedroom through the sliding glass door. She closed the curtains but he could see the lights go on, then the blue color of the television screen just noticeable through the fabric. He would wait until the TV went off then he would walk over to Frederick's lot.

About an hour later, everything went dark at the Craigs. It would only take him five minutes to walk over there and he was certain she wouldn't be able to hear him dropping the pieces of fruit and candy over the fence onto her property. He contemplated whether or not he should go out on his boat tomorrow or watch the festivities from his balcony. She would never suspect him of trying to poison her dog. It was best to be sure, so he would stay home and see if the dog became ill.

CHAPTER 64

August 20 - Monday

Miranda was awakened by a cold, wet snout in her face, Maynard's way of telling her it was time to get up, let him out and feed him. She looked at the clock, six, ugh; she would have loved to sleep another hour, but guessed that was not going to happen. Putting on her robe, she let him out the sliders in her room and went to put on a pot of coffee. She got him fresh water and put his dog food in his dish. Usually, he was at the sliders by the great room by now. She opened the door and yelled for him to come and get his breakfast. She left the door open so he could come in when he was ready. A few minutes later, he ran into the house and wolfed down his food.

So far it was a quiet morning; no construction sounds could be heard. Maynard was on the couch sleeping. All was good with the world.

Miranda made herself a bowl of oatmeal with fresh blueberries and enjoyed three cups of coffee while she read her book at the kitchen table. Checking the clock she saw it was close to nine o'clock. She quickly washed her face and brushed her teeth, got dressed and made the bed. Then she heard something, like retching.

She ran into the back room and found Maynard throwing up all over the floor. Pushing him to the door, she opened it and helped him outside. The mess had to be cleaned up so she grabbed the Clorox wipes and paper towels. Maynard had thrown up many times over the years. When he was about two years old, he had gotten his paws up to the counter and gobbled a whole stick of butter. That resulted in a gross congealed mess. Another time he stole an entire ear of corn and proceeded to eat the corn and the cob. That wasn't fun to clean up either! But it was usually one and done. He would throw it up and be fine. But when Miranda looked outside, he was still throwing up and also having diarrhea. This wasn't good. She would have to get him to the vet.

Trash bags, she thought. I will put down a bunch of big trash bags on his doggy hammock that stretched over the back seat to the front seat of the car. If he continued to be sick at least it will be somewhat contained. Now, the big issue was getting him into the car.

Thankfully, he seemed to pause and Miranda was able to walk him out to the front yard and helped him up into the car. House locked, purse in hand, she got in the car and headed for the nearest veterinarian. Pet Smart was the only one she was aware of and she didn't have time to do an internet search. If they weren't able to help him, they would be able to refer her to someone who could.

Miranda was an absolute blubbering mess when she finally got home about two hours later. The vet had been wonderful, taking control of the situation. They took Maynard into an examination room and hooked up fluids and took some blood samples. He was still sick at times, and they were able to take some stool and vomit samples to analyze. It looked like he had gotten a hold of chocolate and something else, they couldn't tell yet. There was nothing Miranda could do but to go home because they would need to monitor him for at least twenty-four to forty-eight hours. He would probably be alright since she had gotten him there so quickly and he had been throwing up so much of what he had eaten. They were optimistic that he had not fully ingested whatever it was.

Sobbing, she called Jack and told him what had happened as she drove back to the house. He told her he would call the vet later in the day and get an update and call her back. She just needed to relax and be assured the vet would do all he could to save Maynard. They decided not to tell the kids until they got the next update.

Miranda spent the rest of the morning cleaning out the back of her car. Her next mission was to check the entire backyard for the offending food. Nothing. That dog must have eaten all there was!

Jack, as well as the vet, called later to report Maynard was responding well to the treatment and that he should be able to come home tomorrow afternoon.

Exhausted, Miranda didn't want to drive to the library to see Diane so she called. One of the other librarians said that Diane had taken a few vacation days and would return at the end of the week.

She would just have to try to figure it out herself with the help of the internet.

CHAPTER 65

August 20 - Monday

Alek watched with glee as Miranda carried the dog to the car. Later he heard her conversation with Jack and the vet about monitoring the dog until the next day.

Now he just had to get to Frederick's property tonight and find those files. He had a good idea where they were hidden after hearing the quote.

Everyone thought Frederick was strange, raking his rocks. He was out there constantly, pushing the rocks around, pulling up the weeds, bending down to pick them up and throwing them into a bag. He would prune the branches on his shrubs and the grapevines by the Craig's shed. Alek was certain the files were somewhere near that grapevine. It was hidden from view by the other shrubs.

It would be noisy digging around; just walking around on the river rock would create noise and alert her that someone was next door. He needed to take Miranda out of the picture as well.

Later that night, Alek saw Miranda inside the house preparing her dinner. He ran over to her street and quietly climbed over the Craig's fence into their backyard. Hiding in the outdoor shower, he would wait until she came out for a shower or after she went to bed he could break in again through the slider in the back room by the pool.

It was getting dark and Alek was getting impatient. Finally, he heard the sliding glass door open from the bedroom. He climbed on the bench that was just inside the door and pressed his body against the inside wall. She wouldn't see him until it was too late. He would take her by surprise.

Miranda had her arms full with a towel, robe, shampoo, conditioner, a bar of soap, scrubber and a bottle of bleach. It was a struggle to open the shower door. As she walked in, she sensed movement to her left. Before she could take action, she felt a blow to her head.

Alek brought the wooden club down on Miranda's head the minute she walked into the shower. Her body crumpled to the ground and the items fell from her hands. He picked up the towel and wrapped the club while kicking the rest of the items out of the way. Thankfully, she was a smallish woman, and he was able to put her over his shoulder and carry her out of the shower and into the bedroom. It was dark enough that other neighbors wouldn't be able to see what he was doing.

After laying her on the bed, he bound both feet and hands together completely with duct tape and put a piece on her mouth careful to keep it away from her nose. There would be no way she could walk or remove the tape herself. He didn't want to kill her, just keep her out of the way and quiet until he was done with his search. He was certain she hadn't seen him; he was quick and it was very dark inside the shower.

Double checking to make sure all his fingerprints were wiped from the various surfaces, he went back to Frederick's property and began to look for the hiding place near the grapevine.

How stupid he had been to not search the outside, although he probably wouldn't have thought to look around the grapevine. He found a shovel in Frederick's outdoor shed and began to clear away the rocks surrounding the base of the plant. Right there in the front was a metal flap and latch. Taking the sharp edge of the shovel, he rammed it into the latch breaking it. The flap easily opened to expose a large metal box filled with files, papers and flash drives.

Quickly, he removed everything from the box and laid it with the towel wrapped club. He closed the flap and positioned the latch back where it should have been and covered everything with a thick layer of rock. The shovel was put back in the shed after having wiped away his prints. He left with both bundles under his arms. Finally, he would be able to see if Frederick and Chicky had anything on him and lucky to be the one to destroy it.

CHAPTER 66

August 21 - Tuesday

She thought she heard some buzzing. Why wasn't Maynard coming to wake her up like he usually did? There was something she needed to do, but couldn't think of it. Did it have to do with that buzzing? Could she have a tumor? No, she was thinking of that movie *Grandma's Boy*. She needed to make it stop but she couldn't move her arms. Maybe if she stood up she would be able to make it stop. Her legs weren't moving. Why did her head hurt? God, why didn't that buzzing stop?!

The fog began to clear in her head, and she realized something was wrong. She opened her eyes and saw that she was lying on her bed. There was something on her mouth and her arms and legs were bound. Immediately, she started to panic. What had happened? She tried to think back to her last memories. What was the last thing I was doing?

Shower, she was going out to the shower, and she opened the door. She couldn't remember anything after that. Why was she here tied up? What is that damned buzzing?

It wasn't buzzing; it was her cell phone in the kitchen. She had to somehow get up and get to the kitchen and let whoever it was on the phone know she needed help.

Rolling her body off the bed, she began to inch worm her way to the kitchen. Her feet were in such a strange position; she wouldn't be able to hop all the way. Her bound hands and feet were on the floor, she looked like an inverted "V". The hands would move forward a bit, followed by the feet. It would be very slow going, but she would eventually get there.

Whoever put this tape on really did a number on her. Both of her feet were bound together in one big ball, as were her hands. There would be no way she could even pull the tape from her mouth.

She was able to find her phone but unable to use her fingers to press the buttons to dial Jack. Maybe she could use her nose. It took a couple of tries to press the button at the bottom of the screen, then swipe to open up for her apps and functions. Again, she used her nose to press phone, then Jack on the screen of recent calls. When he answered the phone he yelled, "Where the heck have you been? I have been trying to reach you since last night! The vet called and said you could pick up Maynard this afternoon. He had really come around last night and he would be good to go about two o'clock."

Miranda began making noises through the tape. She was frustrated and unable to pull the tape away. Finally, she saw the bottle of hand lotion on the counter. She could wedge the pump under one corner of the tape and hopefully pull it away. After working for a few seconds, she was able to pull enough away from her mouth to talk.

"Jack, please call the police and have them get here as fast as they can. I was hit over the head I think, last night, and I just woke up in my bed with my feet and hands bound. I don't know what happened but I need help!"

Jack yelled to one of his associates to get the Long Beach Township police on the other line and have them rush to their house. He gave the address while he stayed on his phone with Miranda.

About fifteen minutes later, Miranda heard sirens and the sounds of vehicles pulling onto the rocks in the front of their house. She made her way to the front door but was unable to pull it open because she still couldn't get the bindings off her hands and feet. Out front, she saw township police, Barnegat Light paramedics and John Franklin rushing toward the door.

She yelled through the door that she couldn't open it and suggested they try the sliders in the back. Maybe whoever hit her had not been able to lock up after he left.

She heard them opening the sliding glass doors in the back room and John, upon entering the kitchen immediately gave her a hug and helped her to the couch where paramedics began to look her over, especially her head. The bindings were the next things to be addressed and after they were removed, she rubbed her wrists to help the feeling return. She told Jack that help had arrived and that she was alright. He said he would come down as soon as possible, stopping to pick up Maynard on the way.

She explained to the group what she thought happened the night before and John and the police officers went out back to investigate. When they came back in, John said, "We didn't see anything out there other than your shower items on the floor but we will have forensics come out and go over the shower, gate and bedroom areas. Maybe whoever it was got a bit careless and left some telltale evidence. Miranda, do you want to go to the hospital and have your head examined?" After he made that last comment, John looked a bit sheepish and said, "I didn't mean that the way it sounded!"

Miranda, laughed in spite of herself and replied, "No, I just want to find out what is going on. Did you get my message about the letter the Haverford's received from Frederick's lawyer?"

"Yes, we contacted them but unfortunately, the wife threw it away. What a nasty woman she is. She made it sound like it was our fault she received it and that it was such an imposition. But, according to your message, you have most if not all of the quote?"

"Yes, I found it online. Just give me a minute and let me find it on my phone." She handed the phone to John. "I have had a bit of time to think about it. A while back the kids and I had a run in with a raccoon making a nuisance of itself over on Frederick's property. If it hadn't been for that animal, I wouldn't have recognized the vine as a grape vine. I don't think the Steinbeck lines are anything other than to tell Chicky something important is by the grapes."

John read the quote on Miranda's phone, cut and pasted it into an email to himself. Next he called Ray Milford with the Secret Service, telling him what was suspected. He agreed to wait until the teams could arrive and conduct a formal search of the area in order to preserve any evidence they found.

Miranda was starving; she hadn't eaten since about five thirty Monday night. She put on a large pot of coffee and decided scrambled eggs and toast was the easiest. Coffee was offered to the officers; the paramedics had left moments earlier when she refused transport to the hospital. Jack would be there in about two hours so all she could do was eat something and wait.

About the time Jack arrived, the team working on the malware issue arrived. John joined them as they began to photograph then plot out their search, double checking in Frederick's house. They were surprised to see the house was a mess. Someone had been in there at some point and basically took the place apart. One group of agents began to photograph and search the area for any evidence while the other group began digging around the grapevine.

The metal box was found; it too had been destroyed and was completely empty. They were back to square one. Whoever it was seemed to be one step ahead of them at every turn.

John came back into the Craig's house and began to question Miranda about the conversation she overheard at the Haverford's. Who did she tell and when? As she was telling him, John got a funny look on his face and held up a finger to his lips.

A few minutes later, he returned with one of the agents and motioned for him to check the house. A thorough search was completed and three bugs were found and removed from the house.

"Apparently, while you were away, our spy, if you will, figured out we were on to him. For some reason, he targeted you as the best and most likely source of information. Why? Because maybe you are in the thick of it? The fact that Alek lives just over there, has known all the victims, had opportunity and possibly a motive for obtaining the information from those residents who were hacked, and just happens to be Russian born might be enough for us to put him under surveillance. We can tap his phones, get information about his internet activities and we can search his house. I am calling Ray Milford to get the ball rolling. I want someone over there ASAP." As John said this, they all looked over at Alek's house. No boat.

"Did anyone see that boat leave?" John yelled to everyone in Miranda's house. No one saw anything. He ran next door and asked the agents finalizing the search of the property. Nothing was seen. No one had any idea when Alek left.

CHAPTER 67

August 21 - Tuesday

Alek had been up all night reviewing the files and documents Frederick had stored in his underground locker. So many were implicated, including him. There were transcripts of therapy sessions, conversations that were recorded then transcribed, dates, objectives, contacts, plans of sabotage, subterfuge and other deceptions by Soviet agents planted within the United States government and within major corporations. All were patients of Dr. Wasserman.

It was a wide spread web and Frederick and Chicky had been working for decades trying to make sense of it and devise a plan to put a stop to it. They had successes over the years but more and more players were being thrust into the game. The dossiers, once complete, were sent to Homeland Security for follow up.

Alek's dossier was incomplete, but Chicky knew he was guilty of espionage. He knew Frederick had something in mind that night he went to see him after the Craig's party. Luckily, he took action first. He should have been suspicious of the tea. Too late now.

He had to try to destroy what he had, that was the only thing left for him to do. Soon the Craig woman would be found and the police would be all over the neighborhood. He had to assume, something about him and his activities made its way to Homeland Security and it would only be a matter of time before they came for him. It was time to go.

Alek didn't bother to tell his wife he was going out on his boat. She was busy in the kitchen making breakfast or something, so he quickly made his way outside. He had packed a few things, some money, and his passport (although he would never use this one again). He sent an encrypted message using his satellite phone, but hadn't received a message in return. All he could do was hope they would pick him up within a reasonable amount of time.

As he was boarding his boat, his wife ran out yelling, "Alek, you forgot your coffee and lunch! I made your favorite corned beef and Swiss sandwiches." She handed him the lunch bag and waved as he motored off.

The water was calm, and the weather was relatively comfortable for an early August morning. It would be quite pleasant heading out into the ocean this morning; too bad he couldn't relax and enjoy the ride and good weather. He had to make his way quickly, no telling how soon the shit would hit the fan.

Over an hour later, he threw out his anchor and waited. He was quite a ways out in the ocean, in international waters. He plugged in his coordinates into his GPS and sent the beacon so he could be found. Now he waited.

How thoughtful of his wife to make him some food and coffee. He didn't think she was paying any attention to what he was doing. It's too bad he won't be seeing her any more.

He pulled out the thermos of coffee and poured himself a cup, smelling the aroma. He sat down at the helm and drank his coffee.

CHAPTER 68

August 21 - Tuesday

Alek had been watched by another set of eyes for years.
Everything couldn't be left up to one man. No mistakes could be
made that would expose the true purpose of the break-ins and hacks.

Now with two deaths and that Craig woman getting hurt, Alek
was a liability and had to be eliminated.

His boat was spotted up ahead. Checking all around to make
sure there were no other boats in the area, the Bayliner approached
and pulled up alongside, careful to secure fenders in between the two
boats so there would be no scratches or dents. She didn't want to
alert the authorities when they got here that there had been another
boat. Everything appeared to be quiet, Alek couldn't be seen.

Boarding the boat quietly in case the coffee hadn't done the
trick, Alina Pronin, Alek's wife, approached the pilot house. There
she found Alek slumped over the controls. She grabbed him by the
collar and began to pull him out and over to the stern where there
was a door. It wouldn't do for the authorities to find his body
floating in the water. She hunted around the boat until she found a
tool box and line. She tied the line around Alek's feet and then
secured the tool box to line. She opened the door and pushed him out
into the ocean.

Quickly, she picked up the coffee cup and thermos, removed the
food and any other identifying objects. The boat must appear to be
abandoned.

Already his body had sunk deep into the ocean. They wouldn't
start looking for him until she signaled the alarm.

Alina boarded the borrowed Bayliner with the items she had
collected from Alek's boat. Next she had to return the Bayliner to its
rightful berth. Ruth Weinstein and her husband told her the other
day when she was taking her class at the Foundation that they were
returning to Florida earlier than normal this year because of Sol's
health. He preferred his physicians down there and it was easier to

get to and from their Florida house to the doctor offices. Their boat would be dry docked in September as usual and the key hidden aboard for the marina to bring it in.

Alina had known them for years and knew their schedules and habits. It had been easy to walk the few streets over to their house and just get on their boat. No one was watching. She had been anticipating the arrival of the police at the Craig's house when she saw Miranda hobbling around this morning. She laced Alek's coffee and made him some food, knowing he would be running away very soon. She couldn't let him really get away. She needed to put enough drugs in the coffee to knock him out, but not too much that might make him sick and throw up all over his boat. There wouldn't be time to clean it up and get rid of his body.

Silvermaster and Ullmann did not leave things to chance since the fiasco with Elizabeth Bentley. They planned and schemed, setting numerous precautions into place. They had been instrumental in Alek's arranged marriage to Alina. Over the years, Ullmann had helped her in her education and training as a Soviet agent and she had to be kept a secret. No one could be trusted other than Ullmann as to her true identity and purpose.

This would be their true legacy, even though they wouldn't be around to enjoy it.

Russia had concerns that Alek might take things in his own hands and he had. Two murders, albeit necessary, weren't in the plan, at least not yet.

When Chicky started asking her questions, she knew her husband was in trouble. The plans were about to fall apart. She notified her counterpart in Russia and had been given instructions.

What did Alek think she did day in and day out when he was out fishing? Sit at home and twiddle her thumbs? She took classes either online or at the community college. She was more computer savvy than he was. She had been working on her own for years now and probably accomplished much more than he had been able to.

Thank god she was able to keep those people out of her house. She decrypted the data on that hard drive and processor Alek picked up from the transcription agency. It was loaded with incriminating evidence not only about Alek but other Soviet operatives. She had been able to warn them so they could leave the country. She removed every bit of evidence, except that which would incriminate Alek. With him missing, and hopefully assumed dead, they would close the book, thus freeing her up to continue on with her mission.

Now she had to get back, return the boat and begin the show at home. She checked her watch; it was only twelve thirty.

Alina walked into her house, and went straight to Alek's office. Only having a few hours, she went to work. They had to know what he was up to, so she decided to remove just what she needed to finish her mission. He had completed quite a bit of research that would be beneficial to her. She copied the files of interest to her and then attached them to a special email address which would allow her to retrieve it at a later time. She deleted everything pertaining to Oyster Creek.

Next, she had to make an appearance outside to give herself an alibi. A little work in the garden, and a quick cool off in the lagoon. Then right back to work in the office. When the time came, she would begin the worried wife routine looking for her late husband to come down the lagoon.

CHAPTER 69

August 21 - Tuesday

They waited. John was anxiously pacing back and forth on the deck outside the Craig's house. Couldn't bureaucracy move faster just this once?

Miranda made some sandwiches and iced tea and brought it outside for the agents while they waited for clearance to move ahead and search Alek's house. As they were watching the house, Alek's wife came out and looked down the lagoon. She waited a bit, and then went back into the house. It was already five thirty; usually, Alek came back before now. She kept checking every fifteen minutes for his arrival. More time passed. By seven that night, she looked frantic.

John received a phone call from Ray Milford granting him and the other agents' authority to search Alek's house, property and boat. John relayed that Alek and the boat were missing and suggested the Coast Guard be put on alert. But it seemed they were already notified. One of the police officers came out and told the group that a call had just come in from across the lagoon that a Mr. Alek Pronin had been gone all day and was late returning on his boat. The Coast Guard had been notified and was sending out a patrol to search for the missing boater.

With the go ahead, the officers, agents and John went to the Pronin residence and began to question the wife, search the house and the property. They hoped to find what they needed to prosecute.

The search for the missing boater went on all night, additional Coast Guard patrol boats as well as helicopters aided in the effort. The boat was finally found and boarded by officers only to find it empty. The boat was completely empty, no equipment, food, supplies, phone, body, nothing.

CHAPTER 70

August 22 - Wednesday

The call came in that Alek's boat was being towed back to his dock. A forensic team had processed every inch of the vessel and only Alek's fingerprints were on it. That seemed to make sense since he was the one to take it out almost every day to go fishing.

John and a few other agents were waiting at the Craig's, while others were at the Pronin property. There was still a lot of work that had to be done. Mrs. Pronin had been taken in for questioning, but so far she appeared to know nothing about her husband's business or extracurricular activities. They specifically asked her about the office loaded with computer equipment. She told them that she had been forbidden to enter the room and that it was always locked even when he was inside it. He had warned her that his work was highly confidential and it was in her best interest not to pry.

The Goldbergs made it back to the shore just after lunch time. They had heard on the news that a man had been lost at sea and that the search was continuing. There was no mention in the report that it had been Alek or that there was any relationship to the deaths of Chicky Haverford or Frederick Wasserman.

Miranda wondered if the government would try to hush it up and not release the details of the multiple counts of breaking and entering, bugging and hacking of over thirty computers and phones or that he was a suspected Soviet spy. She thought it was an important lesson that needed to be taught. Be observant, pay attention. Know what goes on around you. After 9/11, people were more observant. Apparently, after a few years, complacency sets in.

Later that evening, Lori, John and the Goldbergs joined the Craigs for dinner and copious amounts of wine. This had been an unbelievable experience for all of them, knowing that the United States was close to a potential economic disaster at the hands of the Russians.

John had told them of the plans found in Alek's secret back room. How hackers were taking the data, having access to all those computers and hacking into a multitude of systems. The intent was to be able to take over all the systems, not allowing the companies even to shut down anything. The hackers would have had total control- to create massive blackouts, no communication whatsoever. Transportation- buses, trains, airports, and air traffic control would be unable to operate. There would be no food, gas deliveries, and supplies. They even had a way of shutting down and disabling power generators that supported homes, businesses, hospitals and military forts in the event of an emergency by disrupting the gas lines that supported them.

Liz had told John about what Miranda said early on about their neighbors, where they were from and their ethnic backgrounds. But what was really interesting and what Alek noticed was the occupations and the opportunities that were right at his doorstep.

These people had jobs that gave the hackers access to critical information and to important contacts. What was frightening was that they were all lax in their security as were their companies. This became a real 'Come to Jesus' moment for everyone.

John said, "I think Alek got his own 'Come to Jesus' moment when he realized we were onto him and he decided to take the easy way out by killing himself.

Miranda being the cynic said "I could think up a number of things that could have happened to him."

"One: I agree that he could have committed suicide: Knowing it was only a matter of time before he was caught. Maybe the thought of rotting in an American prison was too much for him."

"Two: He could have had a heart attack and fallen overboard. He was in his seventies I think, maybe older. It was hard to tell, he was quite fit for his age. Maybe he had health issues no one was aware of."

"Three: His lover met him out there and they sailed away on another boat. It was obvious he wasn't enamored with his wife. We would hear them arguing and he was gone most days. He could have had someone he was involved with and she helped him disappear."

"Four: He went overboard to go to the bathroom and Mary Lee ate him. We have been tracking Mary Lee, the shark, all summer and she has been in the waters around Harvey Cedars, so this could be possible."

"Five: He observed drugs or people smuggling and they dragged him off his boat and killed him. I'm sure the Coast Guard can give you information on the drug and people trafficking that goes on along the coast. Who knows what he could have stumbled on out there? If he did, they would have to get rid of him."

"Six: His wife, hating him, hired someone to go after him, kill him then throw his body overboard. Going back to point number three, his wife could have gotten fed up with him and hired someone to take him out so she would have everything minus him."

"Seven: The CIA caught up with him, killed him and removed his body so it would never be found. The CIA has been working on the Soviet problem for decades. They were aware of what Chicky and Frederick found out and decided to use that particular day to avenge their deaths and put an end to Alek, thus tying up a lot of loose ends."

"Eight: The Soviets met him out there, being unhappy he screwed up the plans, killed him. He might have called his handlers and asked for help getting away. They too, wanted to sever the connection between them and killed him so he couldn't bargain his way out of prison like so many seem to do.

"Nine: He rendezvoused with a Soviet submarine and they returned him to Russia. As we know, there have been sightings of Russian subs in these waters and he could have hitched a ride hoping for a second chance.

"Regardless of what happened to him, he, like Silvermaster and Ullmann, got away with it, never to be charged or formally arrested as a spy."

Miranda started to laugh, "It's funny. This all started as a lark, imagining intrigue and seeing hints of something that just wasn't right. But the more we researched the more we realized the possibilities. There are Russian spies in the United States. They are caught frequently. There are escaped Nazi war criminals living right next door. Maybe not next door here, but one was found in

Philadelphia. I guess we will never know the true nationality of Frederick. There are Russian submarines patrolling the Atlantic Ocean mere miles from the Jersey Shore and Russian malware is lurking on computers everywhere. Russia had already set its sights on the Ukraine and used it as test run, preparing them to take us on. They nearly made greater inroads into our economic system this time but luckily were stopped before any real damage could occur."

"I wonder why the reference to the *Grapes of Wrath*? Was it as simple as pointing a finger at the grapevines? Or was he trying to convey a deeper meaning? Was Frederick comparing the Russians to the migrant workers and the United States to the greedy corporations and landowners? Like the migrants in the book, there are many Russians unable to feed themselves and have little hope or optimism. There are references in the book to 'reds' or communism as it relates to the possibilities if workers organize. Are the Russians so plagued by the American Dream that they have to do everything in the power to destroy it? Why not just try to duplicate it?"

CHAPTER 71

August 24 - Friday

Jack called the office and told them he wouldn't be back until after Labor Day. He was not letting Miranda out of his sights. Alek hadn't been found, and who knew if he would show up and finish what he started the other night.

It appeared most of the work had been completed on the Haverford house and it was blissfully quiet.

Most families had gone back to their regular homes, kids were returning to school and college while their folks went back to work. Service at the local restaurants and shops would be lacking without all the kids to help out. But that was alright, those who were still at the shore had nowhere to go and no rush to get there. They were experienced in the end of the summer slowdown and relished the thought of quieter streets and cooler nights.

Jack officially put an end to the eleven o'clock rule until next spring, saying they were doing nothing but enjoy the solitude.

Miranda finally finished the book she had been reading. It had described an appetizer and dinner that sounded delicious. She was able to pick up everything she needed at Antonio's and Whites Grocery Store.

She sliced and toasted the baguette, put a dollop of remoulade sauce on each piece followed by a slice of hard-boiled egg and ending with a fresh marinated anchovy. This would be served with the remainder of a bottle of white wine she had in the refrigerator. For dinner, it would be grilled New York Strip Steaks, medium rare and accompanied by roasted potato wedges and an arugula salad with red onion, tomato, shaved carrots and parmesan cheese. There was one more bottle of Amizetta Complexity 2016; an incredible red wine that would go perfectly with the steaks.

When everything was ready, she put up the umbrella on the outdoor table and they enjoyed their dinner in the warmth of that beautiful August day.

After dinner they called the kids and told them what had happened. They wanted to come home because they were concerned for their mother and what had happened to Maynard. She swore both of them were fine and insisted that they stay where they were. Miranda turned the conversation around and the kids began to tell funny stories about school and their friends. She and Jack were relieved they were doing well and enjoying their time away.

CHAPTER 72

September 3 - Monday

Since Alek disappeared and no body was found, Alina could not declare her husband dead and therefore, unable to sell the boat or the house since they were in his name.

Alina had to stay in Loveladies until the courts decided he was legally dead. That was alright with her, she still had work to accomplish in Loveladies. Thankfully, they had significant savings to see her through the next few years.

The FBI had not discovered what Alek hid in the secret compartments under the floor of his office. She might need the drugs and equipment later.

Homeland Security had interrogated her for hours after Alek's boat had been returned and the house searched. She told them Alek had been a decent husband, providing food and a roof over her head. She had come to the United States from Belarus as a kind of mail order bride; a way to escape the desolation of her homeland with the hopes of a better life. Over the years, Alek worked long, hard hours starting as a construction worker for Silvermaster and Ullmann building homes in Loveladies. He continued a few years after the 1962 Ash Wednesday storm, but was encouraged to begin a new occupation as a researcher for a think tank.

They continued living their quiet life, Alek traveling occasionally for conferences and client meetings. She would stay home, maybe go to the Foundation for a class or lunch with one of her few friends.

Recently, she did notice he was more distracted and took his boat out fishing almost daily. He attended a conference a week or so ago and she found him very irritable when he returned.

No, she did not know the name of the think tank or the nature of his research. Yes, she did know he was Russian born, and that was the reason she agreed to the marriage. She did what was expected of her and agreed to never enter his office. She had been raised to obey and serve her husband; never to question him. That was what a good wife did.

Of course, they did not suspect her because women of her generation and nationality acted that way. They eventually released her and she returned to her empty home.

It had been a long day and she was exhausted. She made herself something to eat and a nice cup of tea. Taking her meal outside, she sat at their table by the lagoon. It was a glorious night, not too hot or humid, quiet and serene. She truly loved it here. She had never experienced a sense of peace anywhere else. Too bad Alek couldn't be here with her. She laughed to herself. She was finally rid of him and she could get down to business; what she had been set up to accomplish.

After she finished her food, she went back into the house and plugged in her laptop and ran a few checks on her system to make sure the Feds were not monitoring her. Updates on the Oyster Creek sale were needed. Thankfully, the Craig woman and her family were headed home for the winter. She had until at least Spring Break before anyone living on this lagoon would return.

The deaths of Chicky and Frederick were inevitable, they knew too much. At least they never suspected her.

Now she could spend more time sitting on the beach, taking more courses at the Foundation or the Ocean County Community College. There was so much to learn and so little time.

CHAPTER 73

September 3 - Monday

The last few days in Loveladies had been grand. The weather was perfect, low eighties during the day and upper sixties at night. Miranda and Jack had been out on the boat, swam in the pool, gone to dinner with the Goldbergs and watched the Perseid Meteor shower outside on the couch at night.

As always, the end of summer was bitter sweet, always coming too soon. They never wanted to leave, but they needed to pack up the rest of the food and their clothes and get back home.

Miranda was driving home with Maynard in the back seat when Jack phoned. He had gotten a call from the property manage at their new apartment building. When the property was transferred to the Craig's LLC, there had been a number of tenants whose leases were expiring. The property manager had contacted a company that would help find individuals who were interested in renting an apartment in their area. This company would do the background and finance check of the potential tenant. It also allowed the renter to pay the rent through direct deposit. They had gotten their first renter through this new service. Two weeks after moving in, the new tenant was found dead in his apartment. The property manager thought something was strange in how the body was found.

THE END

Coming soon, *Deadly Deposit*, the second in the Miranda Craig series.

AUTHOR BIOGRAPHY

Keslie Patch-Bohrod grew up in Ravenna, Ohio. After graduate school, she lived and worked in Orlando, Florida; Macon, Georgia; Atlanta, Georgia; Cranbury, New Jersey; and New York City. Presently, she lives in Warren, New Jersey with her husband Bill and their dog Bo while summers are spent in Loveladies, New Jersey with their two adult children Jaysen and Stephanie.

Contact the author at loveladiesennui@gmail.com and visit her website at https://kesliebohrod.wixsite.com/loveladiesennui

Starry Night Publishing

Everyone has a story...

Don't spend your life trying to get published! Don't tolerate rejection! Don't do all the work and allow the publishing companies to reap the rewards!

Millions of independent authors like you are making money, publishing their stories now. Our technological know-how will take the headaches out of getting published. Let Starry Night Publishing take care of the hard parts, so you can focus on writing. You simply send us your Word Document, and we do the rest. It really is that simple!

The big companies want to publish only "celebrity authors," not the average book-writer. It's almost impossible for first-time authors to get published today. This has led many authors to go the self-publishing route. Until recently, this was considered "vanity-publishing." You spent large sums of your money to get twenty copies of your book, to give to relatives at Christmas just so you could see your name on the cover. However, the self-publishing industry allows authors to get published in a timely fashion, retain the rights to your work, keeping up to ninety percent of your royalties instead of the traditional five percent.

We've opened up the gates, allowing you inside the world of publishing. While others charge you as much as fifteen-thousand dollars for a publishing package, we charge less than five-hundred dollars to cover copyright, ISBN, and distribution costs. Do you really want to spend all your time formatting, converting, designing a cover, and then promoting your book because no one else will?

Our editors are professionals, able to create a top-notch book that you will be proud of. Becoming a published author is supposed to be fun, not a hassle.

At Starry Night Publishing, you submit your work, we create a professional-looking cover, a table of contents, compile your text and images into the appropriate format, convert your files for eReaders, take care of copyright information, assign an ISBN, allow you to keep one-hundred-percent of your rights, distribute your story worldwide on Amazon, Barnes and Noble and many other retailers, and write you a check for your royalties. There are no other hidden fees involved! You don't pay extra for a cover or to keep your book in print. We promise! Everything is included! You even get a free copy of your book and unlimited half-price copies.

In nine short years, we've published more than four thousand books, compared to the major publishing houses, which only add an average of six new titles per year. We will publish your fiction or non-fiction books about anything and look forward to reading your stories and sharing them with the world.

We sincerely hope that you will join the growing Starry Night Publishing family, become a published author, and gain the world-wide exposure that you deserve. You deserve to succeed. Success comes to those who make opportunities happen, not those who wait for opportunities to happen. You just have to try. Thanks for joining us on our journey.

www.starrynightpublishing.com

www.facebook.com/starrynightpublishing/

Made in the USA
Middletown, DE
10 June 2021